E. V. Thompson was born in London and brought up in Oxfordshire. After periods in the Navy and the police force, both in the UK and overseas, he spent many years in Africa, serving as Chief Security Officer in what was formerly the Rhodesian Department of Civil Aviation.

During that time, over two hundred of his stories were published and broadcast, and he returned to England committed to becoming a full-time writer. Moving to Bodmin Moor, he wrote the book that won him the Best Historical Novelist Award for 1977. Its success has been followed by twenty other novels, including the acclaimed *Retallick* family saga and the popular *Jagos of Cornwall* series.

E. V. Thompson continues to live in Cornwall, where he shares a charming house overlooking the sea near Mevagissey with his wife, two sons and a wide variety of family pets.

HERE, THERE AND YESTERDAY

In this collection of short stories by E. V. Thompson, there are tales of the sea: Prunella the cat is in trouble when she's found by the captain of the ship she's hiding on; every time a galleon appears off West Cornwall, a member of the St Gerard family dies — now only Wendy is left, and the galleon reappears . . . And there are stories about criminals: in Arkansas a man is mugged on his way home; three gangsters turn up at the shop of West End fence Elijah Fink to claim their dues . . . And there are other pitfalls: a man, lost on a walking holiday in Ireland, arrives at an isolated house on the moors — and discovers that it's haunted . . .

Books by E. V. Thompson
Published by The House of Ulverscroft

THE MUSIC MAKERS
THE DREAM TRADERS
CRY ONCE ALONE
BECKY
GOD'S HIGHLANDER
CASSIE
WYCHWOOD
BLUE DRESS GIRL
THE TOLPUDDLE WOMAN
LEWIN'S MEAD
MOONTIDE
CAST NO SHADOWS
MUD HUTS AND MISSIONARIES
SOMEWHERE A BIRD IS SINGING
SEEK A NEW DAWN
WINDS OF FORTUNE
THE LOST YEARS

THE RETALLICK SAGA:
BEN RETALLICK
CHASE THE WIND
HARVEST OF THE SUN
SINGING SPEARS
THE STRICKEN LAND
LOTTIE TRAGO
RUDDLEMOOR
FIRES OF EVENING

THE JAGOS OF CORNWALL:
THE RESTLESS SEA
POLRUDDEN
MISTRESS OF POLRUDDEN

E. V. THOMPSON

HERE, THERE AND YESTERDAY

Complete and Unabridged

CHARNWOOD
Leicester

First published in Great Britain in 2000

First Charnwood Edition
published 2003

British Library CIP Data

Thompson, E. V.
    Here, there and yesterday.—Large print ed.—
    Charnwood library series
    1. Large type books
    I. Title
    823.9′14 [F]

    ISBN 0–7089–9367–2

Published by
F. A. Thorpe (Publishing)
Anstey, Leicestershire

Set by Words & Graphics Ltd.
Anstey, Leicestershire
Printed and bound in Great Britain by
T. J. International Ltd., Padstow, Cornwall

Contents

Prunella and the Captain

Her arrival on board was something of a mystery. I would swear she was not with us when we left Devonport dockyard, so it must have happened during our courtesy visit to Falmouth. She seemed so completely at home in the forward mess-deck, I have a sneaking suspicion that one of the Communications ratings had something to do with her presence on board.

It was sheer bad luck that the Commanding Officer discovered her before I did. As the ship's First Lieutenant — 'Jimmy-the-One' or 'Number One' in naval jargon — I was supposed to know about everything that went on in the ship.

We were on our way to carry out oceanographic research in the Aegean Sea, our minesweeper being specially fitted out for the purpose, when the discovery was made.

The Captain had decided to make an inspection of the ship at ten o'clock on Saturday morning. For two hours before the appointed time the ship was a hive of activity. Paintwork was scrubbed, lockers pulled out for every trace of dust to be removed, and the brasswork gleamed like the fittings in a gipsy caravan.

I made a quick check shortly before ten o'clock and was able to report to the captain that all was ready for his rounds.

He began his inspection on the Petty Officers' mess-deck, then proceeded to the seamen's mess and the stokers' living quarters. The latter was always one of the most spotless parts of any ship, despite the stokers' oily, greasy place of work. Finally, we arrived on the Communications' mess-deck, so called because the majority of its occupants were signalmen and telegraphists. The suitcases were neatly stowed on the rack provided for them and not a trace of dust sullied the Captain's finger when he ran it along the top of the fan-shaft. Outside, the sea could be seen heaving gently beyond the sparkling port-holes. All seemed in perfect order. Murmuring his approval, the Captain was about to leave when there was a muffled sound that had nothing at all to do with the normal noises heard on board the ship.

He swung around as though someone had struck him. 'What was that noise?'

The leading signalman in charge of the mess-deck stood rigidly to attention, his gaze fixed on a point above and beyond the Captain's head.

The noise was repeated, this time accompanied by the sound of frantic scratching. Striding past the leading signalman, who was maintaining his rigid pose despite the expression of anguish which had appeared on his face, the Captain went straight to a row of lockers that made up a long seat down one side of the mess-deck. Flinging open the lid of one of them, he paused, looking with disbelief into its depths. Then he reached inside. When his hand emerged there was a half-grown cat dangling by its furry neck between finger and thumb.

Walking slowly over to the leading signalman, the Captain held the protesting animal close to that unfortunate man's face. 'What is this?' he demanded to know.

Only Leading Signalman Brooks's eyes moved. For a fraction of a second they squinted down at the bundle of animated fur, struggling only inches from his nose. Then, flicking upwards, they once more stared into space.

'Er . . . it's a cat, Sir,' he said, vainly hoping that such a positive identification might satisfy the Captain.

'I can see it's a cat!' the Captain hissed. 'What I want to know is what it's doing here on the mess-deck, on my ship?'

He rounded on me, 'Do you know anything about this, Number One?'

I was able to protest my innocence with complete honesty. The Captain looked doubtful for a moment. Then, thrusting the object of his displeasure into my arms, he said, 'Then I suggest you find out — and soon!' With these words, he turned on his heel and strode from the mess-deck.

As the sound of footsteps receded, Leading Signalman Brooks relaxed visibly, but his ordeal was not yet over. Two years of working closely together, and the fact that we were near neighbours in our mutual home town, had brought about a certain informality in our relationship — but I was still the ship's First Lieutenant. Assuming a stern, official voice, I said, 'You heard what the Captain said, Brooks. What is this animal doing on board?'

5

The cat did not help my official manner. She — or 'it', as I then knew the animal — purred happily in my arms and my automatic reaction was to stroke its fur.

Observing this, Leading Signalman Brooks grinned. 'I can't really say how it came on board,' he said. 'A couple of days out from the UK, I woke up in the morning and there she was, curled up in the corner over there. It was as though she belonged. Someone must have been feeding her because she was as fat as butter. I made enquiries, of course, but nobody admitted to knowing anything about her. I'm sorry she's put you on the spot, but we didn't know what to do with her when the Captain carried out his rounds, so we . . . er, *I*, hid her in the locker.'

His clumsy cover-up of the 'we' made it obvious to me that the whole incident was a lower-deck conspiracy. I suspected the Captain and I were probably the only members of the crew who had not been aware of the cat's presence on board.

'You should all know by now that the Captain does not allow animals on board. I'll do what I can for her, but you'll all have to abide by his decision.'

Brooks nodded, but said nothing. Discovering that I was still stroking the offending animal, I hastily deposited her on the deck. She immediately began rubbing herself against my legs, walking in figures of eight in order to include both my legs in her affection.

Reporting to the Captain, I repeated what Brooks had told me. I also added a mild plea for the cat. 'It seems rather a nice animal,' I said. 'And lots of ships in the fleet have pets. Why, I remember hearing that one kept a bear on board. It was the *Manxman*, I believe . . . '

The Captain had extremely bushy eyebrows. He used them now to full effect, peering at me from beneath them with extreme displeasure. 'And I,' he said, icily, 'have heard of a ship that had two of every type of animal . . . *Genesis*, chapter seven, verse nine,' he added, exercising that remarkable penchant for quoting apt portions of the Bible that is the hallmark of a naval officer destined for high office. It also denoted that the Captain had attended Staff College, where a great deal of time is devoted to learning such references.

' . . . However,' the eyebrows became mobile once more, 'had their Lordships at the Admiralty wished me to emulate that well-known gentleman, I doubt very much whether they would have given me command of one of Her Majesty's most modern warships. Kindly inform Leading Signalman Brooks that the cat is to go ashore when we reach Gibraltar.'

The interview at an end, I left the Captain's cabin to acquaint Brooks of the Commanding Officer's decision.

My suspicion that the cat's presence was a conspiracy was confirmed when I overheard whispered enquiries made by seamen, off-duty stokers, and even our newest sub-lieutenant. All were concerned for the fate of the unfortunate feline.

However, I had more important matters to

occupy my time and the incident was soon forgotten. A piece of equipment vital to our research programme had failed at sea. During our brief stay at Gibraltar I needed to work feverishly in order to obtain a replacement and have it fitted before we put to sea once more. It was not until we were actually on patrol in the Aegean that I remembered the cat once more. Even then, it was not exactly a feat of memory that brought her to mind.

I was on watch and happened to look over the edge of the bridge. There, calmly sitting on a hatch cover, carrying out her ablutions, was the cat! Unable to believe the evidence of my own eyes, I turned to Leading Signalman Brooks, who was on the bridge with me.

'Brooks!' I spluttered. 'There's that cat again, sitting out there washing herself. You have deliberately disobeyed the Captain's orders.'

He looked uncomfortable. 'I wouldn't do that, Sir, you know that. It was just . . . well, when we were in harbour, she was nowhere to be found. I thought she must have gone ashore by herself. She turned up again only this morning.'

I rounded on the grinning sub-lieutenant, who immediately assumed an expression more in keeping with the seriousness of the situation.

'Oh my God!' I groaned, 'What is the Captain going to say when he finds out the cat is still on board?'

'Perhaps he won't find out,' said Brooks, hopefully.

I ruled that out immediately. It was my duty to keep the Captain informed of such incidents.

8

Although I dreaded the thought of his reaction, I decided I should tell him right away.

As I anticipated, he was furious.

'Number One,' he roared, pacing angrily up and down the length of his cabin, 'when I give an order on board my own ship, I expect it to be obeyed. Oh yes' — he waved a hand airily in my direction — 'I realise this is only a minor incident — but we must have discipline. *Proverbs* ten, verse four . . . ' He stopped and glared at me. 'You know the quotation, of course?'

When I admitted I did not, the Captain seemed uncertain himself. 'Um! Well, look it up. Look it up. You *should* know it.'

Thinking he had finished with me, I headed for the door, but his voice caught up with me. 'That cat is to be off my ship at our next port of call, wherever it might be. Is that understood?'

Assuring him it was fully understood, I made my escape, hurriedly.

★   ★   ★

We made port much sooner than was anticipated. Orders were received for the ship to call at Skiathos, one of the small islands in the Northern Aegean. Here we were to pick up the wife of the Commander-in-Chief. She had been holidaying there. A lady of notoriously bad temper, it was to be our thankless task to transport her to Istanbul, where the Admiral's flagship, together with the remainder of the fleet, was making a courtesy visit.

9

Our Captain was a confirmed bachelor. The thought of having the Admiral's wife on board for some days put him in a thoroughly bad mood. He gave me numerous instructions concerning the lady's well-being, adding, 'And while we're in Skiathos you can take the opportunity to put that damned cat ashore, too.'

To ensure there would be no slip-up on this occasion, I ordered that the cat — whose name, Brooks informed me, was 'Prunella' — was to be locked in my cabin until we arrived at her future home.

I have to admit, I found Prunella a most entertaining companion. By the time we reached the small bay that forms the harbour for the Greek island I was quite upset at the thought of her imminent departure. Nevertheless, I steeled myself against undue sentimentality. Leading Signalman Brooks was ordered to take the cat on board the boat being sent inshore to pick up the Admiral's irascible lady from the island and dispose of it on land. From his position on the bridge, the Captain witnessed the cat's departure and he gave me a nod of approval.

The boat was inshore for about half an hour. Then I saw it returning, with the Admiral's wife seated at the stern. The Captain joined me at the top of the gangway as we waited for the boat to come alongside.

'Here she is,' he murmured, as the boat bumped against the foot of the gangway. 'The old battleaxe will make our life a misery for the next few days. If I had an Admiral's powers, and a wife like her, I'd organise an Arctic expedition for myself.' Then, with the true hypocrisy of authority, the Captain advanced to meet the lady, a smile of welcome on his face.

Suddenly, he stopped short, the smile freezing. Coming up the gangway was the Admiral's wife. Clasped firmly to her large bosom was Prunella — and the renowned virago was positively drooling!

'Captain,' she cooed, disengaging one hand from Prunella and holding it out limply towards the Commanding Officer. 'How nice to see you. Such a *frightful* island! You can't know how relieved I was to see your ship arrive. And how wonderful of you to send your ship's cat to meet me. I really must tell the Admiral how clever it was of you to remember that I am President of the Naval Cat Club, and founder of Our Furry Friends League.'

The Captain was speechless, but it did not matter. The Admiral's wife never stopped talking. 'You need not be so modest, Captain. Your leading signalman has told me it was entirely your idea. So very kind of you. Not many men with your responsibilities would find time to send a little kitty ashore, in order that she might have a little romp on *terra firma*.'

The grins on the faces of the crew of the launch did nothing to soothe the Captain's acute embarrassment. 'Hrmmph!' he emitted, displaying remarkable aplomb in the circumstances, 'Well . . . we do our best, you know.'

The voyage to Istanbul was, contrary to expectations, idyllic. The Admiral's wife was full of praise for everything on board our ship.

11

Prunella was her constant companion and the permanent purr of the one reflected the mellow mood of the other.

When we arrived at Istanbul, the Admiral's wife seemed almost reluctant to leave us. 'Such a happy ship,' she said, 'But then, from the moment I met Prunella, I knew it would be. A captain with such consideration for a small cat could not fail to be loved and admired by his men. I can't wait to tell the Admiral all about you — and, Captain, I absolutely insist that you have dinner with us on the flagship, this evening.'

Our Captain saluted as the launch carried her away from the ship. Then, taking out a large handkerchief, he wiped perspiration from his brow.

'Remarkable!' he exclaimed. 'Astounding! The last time we met, she castigated me for dropping cigarette ash on her carpet.'

He looked at me suspiciously, 'Were you smiling, Number One?'

I hurriedly assured him it was no more than a mild touch of indigestion.

'Hm!' He was not completely reassured. 'Well . . . in view of the rather extraordinary circumstances, I suppose we had better keep that cat — Prunella, I believe she is called. The Admiral's wife wants me to write an article about her for some cat magazine.'

He stomped away, but paused after taking only a few paces.

'Number One!'

'Sir?'

'Make certain the damned animal is kept

aboard whenever we're in harbour, you know what it says in the Book.'

'Sir?'

'*Genesis* nine, verse seven. Look it up, Number One.'

Biblical footnote:

Genesis 7, verse 9: 'There went in two and two unto Noah into the ark, the male and female, as God had commanded Noah.'

Proverbs 10, verse 4: 'He becometh poor that dealeth with a slack hand.'

Genesis 9, verse 7: 'And you, be ye fruitful, and multiply; bring forth abundantly in the earth, and multiply therein.'

The Luck of the Irish

The road ahead of me twisted and doubled back on itself as it dropped down from the mountains to a green and fertile valley. It was a typical secondary Irish road, but its vagaries caused me little concern now. No longer in a hurry, I had time to admire the scenery about me.

I had crossed the border from Eire during the early hours of the morning and caught up with a few hours sleep in a lay-by beside a small wood. Now, feeling quite refreshed, I was on my way once more. Glancing at my watch I saw it was now three o'clock in the afternoon. Plenty of time to reach Belfast and catch a ferry to take me to Liverpool. I looked at the view appreciatively. The fresh green hills sparkled in the afternoon sun and the trees moved gently, in time to the rhythm of a light breeze. I sighed contentedly. It was good to be alive on such a day as this.

At that moment the road took a sharp turn to the left. As I slowed down and changed to a lower gear, I noticed an old and battered saloon car, nose-down in the ditch beside the road. I immediately applied my brakes — and it was well I did so. Waving his arms frantically, a thick-set little man shot out from behind the car like a startled rabbit, straight into the road in front of me. The moment I came to a halt he ran to my window and I wound it down in order to talk with him.

'Thank the Lord,' he said breathlessly. 'You're the answer to a prayer. I'm in a small spot of bother, you see.'

'I'll be glad to be of assistance,' I began uncertainly. 'But I'm on my way to catch a ferry and in a bit of a hurry . . . '

The remainder of my explanation faded away as a second man appeared from the ditch. A large bank satchel was slung over his shoulder and, in his right hand, he carried an extremely dangerous looking automatic pistol.

The little man grinned. 'I can see by the expression on your face that you'll be happy to help two poor souls in distress. I'm very glad. I hate violence. Cried like a babe, I did, when Michael here had to shoot the bank messenger. Such a terrible pity.'

Michael was apparently one of those strong, silent types. He scowled and waved the gun towards the back of the car. I leaned back and opened it hurriedly. Michael waited for the smaller man to enter the car, then climbed in beside him. Closing the door, he unhitched the bag from his shoulder and placed it carefully on the floor at his feet.

During the whole of the time he was doing this the automatic never wavered and I was looking straight down its barrel.

'A lovely car you have here, sir,' said the talkative one. 'It has plenty of room in the back. As we'll be travelling together for a while, we'd better introduce ourselves. My friend is

18

Michael — and you can call me Paddy.' Without pausing, he continued, 'Now, if you'll just turn the car around, I'll show you a nice quiet little road that crosses the border. Before you even know it we'll be in the Republic. No police or Customs men — and a lovely drive it is too.'

Every so often a man finds himself thrown into the company of those with whom he has nothing in common. When this happens it is much better if he remains silent. This was just such an occasion, yet I felt obliged to air what was on my mind.

'I don't particularly want to cross the border. I came north only this morning.'

'Well, there's a pity! I'm afraid you have no choice in the matter. We're going *south* and we have need of your company. Besides, we don't want you going off and having a little chat with the police now, do we?'

There was nothing I could do. They held all the aces — not to mention the automatic! Starting the car, I turned it around and headed back the way I had come.

As I drove, Paddy kept up a constant stream of chatter. He seemed to be a remarkably knowledgeable man. He told me the history of each district through which we passed, listing the best crops to grow and why. More often than not each gem of wisdom was accompanied by an amusing anecdote. At least, *he* thought them amusing. I found myself unable to capture the same mood.

He also threw in the occasional direction: 'We'd best be taking the next turning left,' or,

'Will you turn right just before we reach the next village? That's where Father Sweeney was shot in the church by the Black-and-Tans. All because he conducted Mass with a rifle tucked beneath his cassock. God rest his Irish soul!'

Before long we turned off the road and followed a cart track that wound around numerous small copses on its way up through the hills. We had covered about twenty miles, bumping alarmingly over ruts and potholes along the way, when I was ordered to stop alongside a gate which opened on to a field. It looked just like a hundred other gates we had passed, but Paddy went into ecstasies about it.

'You'd never believe it,' he burbled happily. 'All we have to do is drive through this field and when we reach the other side we're in God's own country. No fuss or formalities. Can you tell me of any other country in the world where you have less trouble getting in? It's a wonderful place, to be sure.'

'Now you're here you won't be needing me any more,' I said, hopefully.

'What a funny fellow you are! And there's me thinking we'd become good friends. I'm sorry, but we'll be needing your services for a while yet. I'm not keen on the driving and Michael doesn't drive at all. I should hate your beautiful car to end up like the last one. Just wait while I open the gate, then you drive through like a good lad.'

On the far side of the field we passed through a gateway little different from the first one, but now we were in Eire.

Darkness fell soon after this and we drove

20

through the night in comparative silence. We stopped once at a village garage, but I was not able to leave the car. Paddy got out and paid for the petrol. Anticipating such a stop, I had formed a half-hearted plan to make a break for it. This was the point at which Michael made up for his previous silence and also proved to be something of a mind reader.

I was gathering courage for my move when I felt the hard prod of the gun through the back of my seat. Michael uttered the only two words I was to hear from him during the whole journey. The way he growled, 'Keep still!' froze me completely. Apart from the hair on the back of my neck, I did not move a muscle until Paddy returned.

For much of the night we drove through a maze of lanes. I was thoroughly lost by the time Paddy stretched, yawned noisily and said, 'My friend, I've enjoyed this drive very much indeed. However, the time has come for us to part company. Take the next turning to the right and you'll find a lovely country lane. Peaceful it is, with not a house for twenty miles until you come to Killikenny.'

Fortunately, Paddy did not notice my involuntary start at mention of Killikenny. He continued talking.

'As you've been most obliging, I'll tell you what we'll do. In Killikenny we've made our own travel arrangements. We'll drop you here and I'll drive your car very carefully to Killikenny and leave it there for you. I'm afraid it'll be a long walk, but I'm going to give you a couple of hundred pounds from the bank bag. For your trouble, you understand?'

Pointing to a spot where the lights picked out a tree, Paddy said, 'If you'll pull to the side there, we'll settle our business and be on our way.'

I did as I was told. A few minutes later I was standing in the lane clutching two bundles of banknotes, watching the lights of the car disappearing into the distance.

I stood thinking for a few minutes. Then I put the money in my jacket pocket, shrugged my shoulders and turned around to walk back the way we had come. I remembered passing a small country inn about fifteen miles back. That would suit me nicely. In no particular hurry, I reached the inn mid-morning. I was footsore and weary, but a good meal set me up. After taking a bath, I tumbled into bed.

It was a wonderfully peaceful inn and I slept the clock around, not waking until breakfast-time the following morning.

A very appetising meal of bacon, eggs and toast was served to me by a pleasant, rosy-cheeked country girl. At my request, she went off to find me a morning paper. By the time she returned I had finished the meal and was on my second cup of coffee. Opening the paper, the headline caught my eye immediately. 'DARING JEWEL THIEVES CAUGHT,' it read. Beneath, in smaller print, was 'Police puzzled by actions of two burglars'. I read on.

Police are puzzled by the actions of thieves who broke into the Killikenny home of the Dowager Duchess of Grosvenor and escaped in the Duchess's own car after stealing jewellery worth more than two hundred thousand pounds. Despite a country-wide search no trace was found of either car, or culprits. When the police had accepted that the thieves must have made good their escape, two men were seen to drive the stolen motor car into Killikenny. They parked it not two hundred yards from the Duchess's home.

The two men were arrested without a struggle, even though one was later found to be carrying a gun. Most of the missing jewellery has been recovered intact, from the boot of the car.

It is believed the men are also wanted in connection with an armed robbery carried out in Northern Ireland, during the course of which a bank messenger was shot and seriously wounded.

I closed the paper, folded it and placed it upon the table. Putting a hand in my pocket, I felt the two packets of banknotes and smiled. In my other pocket was a valuable diamond necklace and half a dozen rings set with very large precious stones. True, it was not two hundred thousand pounds, but it was certainly better than nothing. What was more, two dangerous men had been arrested.

This gave me particular satisfaction. Like Paddy, I too am a peace-loving man. I deplore criminal violence.

Have This One on Me

Longhorn City was not as large as many of the other cow towns in Arkansas, but there was no disputing the fact it was the wildest. Few sheriffs remained for longer than a month. Some were in office for much shorter terms. The lucky ones rode out of town — in a hurry. The others had a special section of Boot Hill, their tombstones paid for by the citizens of the town. When night fell over Longhorn, decent citizens who lived on the south side of the railway track bolted their doors and shuttered the windows. Once secure in their houses, they tried to ignore the wild whooping, ribald singing and sporadic gunfire that issued forth from saloons and bawdy-houses on the north side of town.

It was very rare indeed for little Caesar Bonicelli to be abroad after dark, but today he had been working later than usual. The sun had quit the sky for more than an hour as he hurried from the rough side of Longhorn City. Muffled up against the cold wind in his overcoat and scarf, the brim of his Eastern-style hat pulled low over his face, he hurried along the boardwalk. Occasionally he would step down to the dirt road, preferring the dangers of unseen potholes to the uncertain mood of a drunken cowboy.

He breathed a sigh of relief when he left the last saloon behind him and saw the railway lines glinting in the light of a rising moon. Few merrymakers strayed this far. There was more fun to be had where there were lights and music.

Caesar Bonicelli's relief was short-lived. As he reached the last building, a stable, a man stepped out of the shadows ahead of him.

Caesar changed direction in order to bypass the man, only to find the other man had done the same.

He stopped and for the first time saw the gun held in the other man's hand. Licking lips which had suddenly become dry, Caesar spoke, nervousness making his Italian accent more pronounced than it would otherwise have been.

'Wh-what — what you want with me?'

'Well now,' said the other man, towering above him. 'In a manner of speaking, I suppose you might say I'm looking for a loan.'

'I . . . I'm sorry. I no give the loans.'

'In that case,' drawled the other man, 'I guess I'll just have to help myself.'

His hand reached forward to the top button of Caesar's overcoat. As the little man drew back, the barrel of the revolver came up to stare him in the eye.

'That's better,' said the big man as Caesar submitted to having his coat unbuttoned. 'What's the matter, you cold? You're shivering fit to bust.'

He felt inside Caesar's jacket and pulled out his wallet. It was bulging with notes.

The big man whistled quietly. 'Whee! You're sure loaded, little man. There's more money here than I've seen in a very long time. I guess I chose the right man to stop.'

28

'Please,' Caesar pleaded, 'That is all the money I make in one month. It is for my wife and the children.'

'Judging by the amount in here you must have a mighty good business. You'd better make do with what you have left over from last month.'

'I beg you ... ' Caesar was almost in tears. 'Half my money is sent to my mother in Italy. Do not take it.'

'Well now, I wouldn't want it said that Butch Donner was a harsh man.' The big man peeled a couple of notes from the wallet. 'Here's ten dollars to send to her. Tell her it's a present from me.'

Putting a hand to his hat brim in salute, Butch Donner moved back in to the shadows and disappeared.

That night there was much wailing and crying emanating from the house occupied by the Bonicelli family.

★　★　★

The following morning, Butch Donner rose late and, in the mirror, examined the rough stubble on his face. He was well satisfied with himself. The previous evening he had sat in on a card game and considerably increased the size of his ill-gotten bankroll. He would find a barber, have a shave and a haircut, then set out to spend his money on a wild spree such as Longhorn City had seldom seen.

He chose the nearest barber shop, stomped inside and seated himself in the first of three chairs. Leaning back, he closed his eyes and prepared to enjoy this unaccustomed luxury.

'Gimme a shave and a haircut,' he said, as he felt the cloth pinned about his neck.

A hand on his forehead gently pushed his head back farther and farther, until it became uncomfortable. Opening his eyes to complain, he jumped in surprise. The movement brought his throat into contact with the super-sharp edge of a cut-throat razor.

'Mr Donner!' said Caesar Bonicelli, his dark eyes glinting. 'You have come to return the loan, no?'

When Butch Donner tried to speak, the effort caused his Adam's apple to bob up and down. When he felt the razor nick his skin, he moaned instead.

Smiling happily, Caesar reached down to Butch Donner's bulging breast pocket and removed the heavy bundle of notes.

'So! It *is* returned with interest. This is too kind of you, Mr Donner.'

Putting the roll in his trouser pocket, he called over his shoulder to his brother, who had been hovering nervously at the back of the shop.

'Alfonso, please call the sheriff. Tell him I have business for him.'

Events moved swiftly after that. The sheriff, accompanied by two hastily sworn-in deputies, came to collect Butch Donner. Before leaving the barber shop, he told Caesar there was a substantial reward out for Donner, for armed robbery.

At the doorway of his shop, Caesar stuck a ten

dollar bill into the outlaw's pocket and beamed at him.

'This is to show that I too am a generous man, Mr Donner. What is it you people say? Ah, yes — please, have this one on me.'

The New Broom

'But . . . I need the work in order to live!'

Tom Phelan's voice held an urgent note of pleading as he faced the two men across the polished desk top in the works office.

The works manager shifted position in his chair, uncomfortably.

'Mr Phelan, I don't think you realise what is involved in this type of work. You have spent your life in an office, most of it in quite a senior position. The post you are applying for is manual work. It entails eight hours of back-breaking slogging. Quite apart from any other consideration, I am not at all convinced that you would be capable of such physical work.'

'Well at least give me a chance to show what I can do,' Tom pleaded. 'I know I'm no longer a young man, but I am perfectly fit and quite able to do a hard day's work. It was not my idea to retire at fifty-five, but new company policy.'

'I don't know, I'm sure.' The works manager's expression registered his indecision.

He turned to his companion, 'What do you think, Mr Harris?'

The third man in the office was about Tom's own age. He shrugged his shoulders.

'I don't know. He *might* be able to do the work. I can recall a man of more than sixty who did the job for years before he moved away from the district to live with his daughter. I can't see

35

any harm in giving Mr Phelan a chance, at least.'

The works manager conceded defeat. 'All right, if you say so. You're the personnel manager. But I'll be quite honest with you, Mr Phelan. After forty years of office work, I believe you will find sweeping too much for you. You'll be working ankle deep in china clay dust — and it's not light work. You'll be expected to pull your weight on equal terms with younger, stronger men.'

'I'll do it, you'll see. There will be no cause for complaint about my work.' Tom was enthusiastic in his relief at being taken on. 'When do I start?'

'On Monday. Morning shift. That's seven o'clock. You'll work seven to three. Give your details to the man in the outer office. That's all, thank you, Mr Phelan.'

Tom left the manager's office holding himself erect. Shoulders thrown back, he was doing his best to shrug off his fifty-seven years. His step was springy with the sheer jubilation of finding work at last.

★   ★   ★

Mary Phelan did not share his happiness.

'But . . . *sweeping*, Tom. I don't mind, of course, you could be a dustman for all I care — if I knew you would be happy doing it. But it's not what you've been used to.'

'Now, don't you start having doubts, Mary. I had the devil's own job convincing the works manager I was capable of doing it. Besides, we desperately need the money. It was silly of us to buy all that furniture for the front room on hire purchase. When I needed to get a new engine for the car, it was the final blow. My pension is not enough to meet our commitments. At our present rate we would run through our capital in six months. Applying for money from the Social Services would be far more humiliating than sweeping floors for a living. I would never be able to hold up my head among my friends.'

'Oh well, you know best, I suppose.' The tone of Mary Phelan's voice implied nothing of the sort.

'Of course I do. Why, if I'm earning again we might even be able to afford a holiday next year. We'll go back to our favourite little place in France . . . '

★ ★ ★

On Monday morning, at ten minutes to seven, Tom was waiting outside the shift foreman's office, inside the works. A tired-looking man wearing a white coat came from the shadows at the back of the building and saw him standing there.

'Are you morning shift?'

'Yes.' Tom felt like a young boy starting at a new school. 'It's my first day. Are you the shift foreman?'

'Not for your shift. Your foreman is away sick. He'll be off all this week. You really ought to have someone to show you around, but we're so short of men it won't be possible. You'll need to manage the best you can. Go down the road and you'll see a big shed marked with a number five. There'll be a broom, shovel and wheelbarrow in there somewhere. It's noisy and it's dusty, but that's the way things are here. Your job is to clear up all the dust and clay that drops from the conveyor belts and driers. Tip it into the sluice at the far end of the shed, so that it can be recycled. You can work in number five for the rest of the week and see your own shift foreman when he comes back. Got that?'

Tom nodded.

'Good. Away you go now. Your meal-break is from twelve o'clock to half-past. Remember, although we don't expect the floor to be spotless, we do expect you to keep it as clean as possible and stop the dust and clay from building up too much.'

With that, Tom Phelan was dismissed from his mind. The shift foreman turned away and went inside his office.

Tom walked down the works road until he reached a large, hangar-type building marked with a white number five. He needed to pick his way along the road carefully. It had rained during the night and the rain had combined with a heavy film of china clay dust to create a dangerously slippery surface.

As Tom walked in through the high doorway of number five, he left the normal world behind and entered what could have been a movie-set for a mechanical Hades.

Three of his five senses were immediately assailed. The clatter and chatter of conveyor belts and the hum of the motors that drove them vied with the roar and rumble of huge cylindrical drying-furnaces, rotating above his head to assault his eardrums. He was overawed by the sight of seemingly endless belts conveying clay and clay dust here, there and nowhere. Towering high above him were giant washing plants that hissed water alongside furnace-heated drying cylinders, the size of Underground trains. Over everything hung a huge pall of dust. It settled inches deep at his feet, tasting dry and acrid to his unaccustomed palate as he breathed it in through his nose.

It seemed impossible that one man could be expected to clean such a vast area. However, remembering the night-shift foreman's words, he set off in search of the implements of his new, unskilled trade. He found them tucked away behind a concrete pillar. There was a double-width broom, a long-handled shovel and a wheelbarrow.

Trundling the squeaking, battered wheel-barrow to the far end of the building, he passed along the way numerous small heaps of clay, shed from defective conveyor belts or sifting machines. Wryly, Tom thought that Hercules must have had similar thoughts to his own when he first surveyed the Augean stables. However, unlike Hercules, he could not divert a river to perform his task for him. He had only a broom and a shovel.

With these, Tom did his back-aching best. He swept the clay dust into great, white-grey piles before shovelling it into the wheelbarrow and trundling it away to a waste-chute in a corner of the building. After a while he learned not to look over his shoulder as he worked. It was discouraging to watch a film of dust settling on the newly-swept floor only a pace or two behind him.

He had most trouble with the heaps of clay. The pieces fused together to form solid, heavy hillocks which needed to be chopped up with the shovel in order to cut them down into more manageable blocks.

Then, when he had swept more than half of the floor area, Tom came across a sight that caused his jaw to drop in utter dismay.

There was a fault at one of the joints of an overhead drier. As the giant machine turned, a shower of heavy clay pellets cascaded to the floor below. The steady stream reminded Tom of wheat pouring from a combine-harvester — but it was the size of the heap of clay pellets that staggered Tom. It was as high as a tall man and covered an area the size of his sitting-room at home.

Unused to manual labour, Tom's unconditioned muscles were already protesting. To be suddenly confronted by this veritable mountain of clay was almost more than he could take.

Then he thought of his seriously depleted bank balance and accepted the inevitable. If it had to be shifted he would manage it somehow. First he would complete his sweeping. Then he could devote the remainder of the working day to this monumental task.

As he swept, his gaze returned with ever increasing frequency to the heap of clay pellets.

It seemed to loom larger with each glance.

The sweeping finally done, he wearily gripped the handles of the ancient wheelbarrow and pushed it to the huge clay pile. He was very tired but did his best to dismiss his complaining muscles and attacked the clay mountain with as much vigour as he could muster.

It was hard work and his tiredness was revealed in the way a full shovel of clay would often twist in his grasp, depositing its load on the floor. Yet Tom kept at it. By the time the shrill whistle sounded for the end of the shift, he had not moved a third of the pile and still it poured down from the defective drier.

Tom said very little to Mary about his day's work and she did not question him. Not even when he made an excuse to go upstairs to bed a full hour before his usual bedtime.

The following morning, when he arrived at work, he went straight to the clay pile. He discovered it was even larger than it had been on the previous day. With a feeling akin to desperation, he set to work on it straight away. He worked until his aching back muscles forced him to stop and he suffered agony when he tried to stand upright. He then began sweeping, but with great haste, in order that he might return to the heap of clay before the shift came to an end.

When the whistle sounded today, he surveyed the results of his labours, both hands supporting the small of his back. Yes, there was no doubt it. He had moved more than on the first day.

Every evening that week he returned home feeling he had almost beaten what had become

41

his *bête noire*. Unfortunately, during the night shift, all his efforts were undone. He found it looming as large as ever in the morning.

By Friday he had arrived at a firm decision. Today, come what may, he would win. Before he went home at the end of the day he would have cleared the giant pile of clay. His week of physical labour had left him aching and tired, but his will was far stronger than the discomfort he felt. The sweeping of the floor was the merest perfunctory formality. The heap of clay was the only thing that really mattered. He shovelled at it savagely, over-filling the wheelbarrow in an attempt to cut down the time wasted when he was not actively attacking his inanimate enemy. Staggering wearily, he weaved an erratic course to the waste-chute with the over-loaded wheelbarrow. It had become an obsession with him. Something to be defeated before he could feel wholly a man once more.

Late in the afternoon he looked at his watch, wiping away the perspiration that blurred his vision. There was half an hour left. Thirty minutes in which to win his self-declared battle.

He redoubled his efforts, the breath rasping from his throat. He scarcely noticed when he collided heavily with supports and machinery during his rubber-legged race to the waste-chute with the groaning wheelbarrow.

When the works whistle blew he estimated there were no more than two wheelbarrow loads to be carried. Then victory would be his.

He completed the task.

More tired than he had ever been in his life

before, he closed his eyes and rocked back on his heels in elated relief. After this, no man would ever be able to say that he, Tom Phelan, was too old for the job. He had beaten it.

He felt the perspiration running in rivulets down his backbone. There was a pounding in his head and a roaring sound in his ears too, but it did not matter. Nothing mattered now. He had proven himself.

He was passing the security man at the works gate when the pain in his chest began. It was so severe he clutched at it, crying out in his agony as the roaring in his ears increased in intensity and overtook him.

The security man caught him as he staggered and fell. With the help of two homeward-bound workers, he carried Tom inside the gate-house.

An ambulance arrived within ten minutes but when the driver felt for a pulse there was nothing. The ambulance driver shook his head.

'He's dead, poor old chap,' he said. 'It must have been a heart attack.'

★ ★ ★

The usual shift foreman was back at work on Monday. He took a husky, young, newly-employed man around number five shed, pointing out the work that needed to be done.

At the heap of clay pellets beneath the drier, the young man stopped.

'What about all this stuff here? Have I got to shift this lot?'

The shift foreman looked from the pile of clay to the young man.

'Don't be a fool. We get a mechanical shovel in to move that. What do you want to do? Kill yourself?'

Here Lies a Hero

It was peaceful in the small country churchyard, the day warm and pleasant. A day to commit to memory and recall from time to time, without remembering how few like it there really were. A temperate breeze bowed rust-coloured heads of the tall grass and gently rustled the ivy that formed a rich tapestry on the churchyard wall. Bumble bees, searching in vain for nectar among the drooping flowers on a recent grave, droned monotonously.

I should not have gone there. I realise that now. There was no reason for the visit. No purpose behind it. Nothing but a rather morbid curiosity. After all these years of trying to forget, I had returned to see what they had inscribed upon his tombstone.

I did not even know where his grave was, but it was not difficult to find. It was, as I knew it would be, an expensive marble tombstone, decorated with ships and angels of mercy.

I read the inscription, carved in deep bold letters: 'John Summers. Died 2nd October 1949 aged 34 years, in a brave attempt to fetch help for others in distress. Greater love hath no man.'

I nodded to myself. Yes, that was what I thought they would have put. John had always been the sort of man of whom others made heroes.

It had always been the same, even at school. A

great swimmer, when John gained a place in the county water-polo team he became the idol of the village. Even Sally my sister, who I had thought to have more sense, fell for him. When I made some comment about it she nearly snapped my head off. 'You're jealous, that's your trouble. How far can *you* swim?' She had me there. Whatever I did in the water made little difference. I travelled in only one direction — straight down.

That was one of the reasons I joined the army when the war came. John Summers, of course, joined the Royal Navy. He became a diver, I believe. Whatever it was, he did it very well, becoming mixed up in just about everything that happened. I never actually *saw* any of his medals, but I used to hear him talking a lot about them.

My war was a very brief one, although I got as far as North Africa before a wayward shell had me sent back to England. I was discharged from the army with a permanently stiff leg. Until the war ended, it did not bother me too much. There was such a general shortage of manpower that nobody bothered about my leg. With the small pension I received, I managed quite well. Then the war came to an end. Suddenly there were more men than there were jobs and I found I was well down on the list of employable men.

John Summers, on the other hand, landed a wonderful job, one that made him the envy of the whole community.

Ours was more a fishing village than a holiday resort, but one millionaire decided he wanted to be different and berthed his yacht there. It wasn't big, I suppose. Not as millionaires' yachts go, anyway. But there was enough on board to make it a delightful little piece of floating luxury — and John Summers was its skipper. The owner came down only a couple of times a year to take the boat out. Nevertheless, John was paid a full year's wage for keeping it seaworthy and doing the odd bit of painting and polishing.

It was a job that suited him very well. On most days you could find him sprawled out in one of the chairs in the local pub, his white cap tilted at a jaunty angle over one eye. He was still an impressive man as far as size went, but he had begun to run to fat and did little exercise to keep it down.

One day — it was October the second, 1949 — he was in the pub as usual. I too was enjoying a lunchtime drink. It was a rare treat for me but, as a result of a medical examination, I had been awarded a slightly larger pension and received a substantial amount of backdated allowance. John and I were the only customers in the pub. All the other village men were out at sea, chasing a large shoal of herrings that had suddenly appeared off the coast. 'Running before a storm,' the old men said. They were probably right. The herrings always appear along our part of the coast when a big blow is due.

Anyway, while we were in the pub I looked out of the window in time to see a Rolls Royce car turn the corner at the end of the road. It glided down to the jetty and the berth where the millionaire's boat was kept.

John was in the middle of a story about the

time he was diving somewhere off the Malayan coast, when I interrupted him.

'Hey, John! Isn't that your employer who's just arrived in a Rolls Royce?' He swung around so quickly that some of his beer slopped out of the mug and down the front of his jersey. My surmise must have been correct. John put down his beer without a word, leaped to his feet and hurried down to the jetty, rubbing at the beer on his jersey with his handkerchief.

His employer was handing a smartly dressed young girl from the car. About half his age, she appeared to be all bottom and tight trousers from where I was sitting. They went aboard the yacht and disappeared down a hatch to the living quarters. Shortly afterwards, the owner reappeared and stood talking to John for a while. John raised his hat and scratched his head, as though he was thinking about something. Then he pointed in the direction of the village. After a few more words, he hurried down the gangplank and began striding towards the pub. He stopped in the doorway and called out to me. 'Hey, Harry? Would you like to earn yourself a few quid?'

'Depends what it's for,' I replied. 'If it's honest and not too difficult I wouldn't mind.'

'It's my boss,' said John. 'He wants to take his latest girlfriend out for a couple of days' trip, just up the coast a little way. Charlie Simmons usually comes as crew, but he's out with the fishermen. So, it seems, are all the rest of the men in the village. You're about the only one left. How about it? You'll do it, won't you?'

I wasn't too sure. You can hardly live in a fishing village without learning how to handle most types of boat, but I had not been out — not as crew that is — since I injured my leg.

'I don't know, John,' I said, 'It's a long time since I went to sea. What's he paying?'

'A fiver a day, and all found. Not only that, if the old man enjoys the trip he'll probably cough up with another twenty at the end of it. He's not mean with his money. Is it a deal?'

I nodded, 'It's a deal.'

He was relieved. 'Good. Go on home and throw a few things in a bag. I'll see you on the yacht in about half an hour. There are a few things I need to buy first.'

Half an hour later I limped up the gang-plank with a few suitable clothes in a small holdall. John was talking to the owner of the yacht, Mr Hardcastle, and he introduced us.

Hardcastle inclined his head in the direction of my leg. 'War wound?'

I nodded.

'I thought it must be. How did you get it? In the navy, I suppose?'

'No, the army. Royal Artillery.'

He raised an eyebrow, 'Army, eh? Well, I hope you know how to handle a boat.'

'I've lived in a fishing village all my life,' I replied, none too graciously. 'It'd be a damn funny thing if I didn't.'

To my surprise, he laughed. 'Aye. I suppose I asked for that.'

Turning to John, he said, 'Right, we'll leave as soon as you are ready. I'll be down below with

51

Miss Meredith. Give us a shout when we're leaving the bay.'

We used the motor to take us clear of the breakwater, but once in the open sea we raised the sails and scudded along in a fairly stiff breeze.

It was a beautiful boat to handle. Everything about it was designed to obtain maximum performance with minimum effort. In fact, a typical luxury yacht. Although there were only two of us crewing, we were not overworked.

As we made our way along the coast the wind became stronger and clouds began to build up ominously behind us.

I had been expecting it. The herrings are seldom wrong.

I pointed the clouds out to John Summers.

'I've been watching them,' he said. 'Don't worry, the boss wants us to put into a cove for the night anyway. I know a nice one not too far away. Another hour's sailing and we'll be there.'

It was less than an hour when John told me to lower the sails. We were going in to the cove under power. Mr Hardcastle, dressed in a thick white fisherman's jersey, helped us.

Miss Meredith — her Christian name was Janet and on closer acquaintance I had decided she was closer to a third of Mr Hardcastle's age — tried to assist. She succeeded in convincing us all that she was the original dumb blonde. Had she not been helping I swear it would have taken us no more than fifteen minutes to have everything secured and stowed away. As it was, it took us thirty.

By this time we were in the cove and John had cut the engine and put out an anchor.

When I had the time to look at our anchorage for the first time I did not like what I saw. For one thing, the entrance to the cove was too narrow. If the storm really blew up in the night and we had to leave in a hurry, it would be extremely difficult to negotiate the gap between the rocks. Not only that, although the land side was well sheltered, it was the wrong side. The wind was coming off the sea. On this side the rocks were low and spray-swept. A heavy sea would break over them with no effort at all.

I said nothing while Mr Hardcastle and the blonde were on deck, but as soon as they had gone below, I voiced my misgivings to John.

He did not take it very kindly.

'Look, Harry,' he said, 'You're just along the for the ride and getting well paid for it, see? I'm the skipper here and I'm quite happy, got that? Right, now go below to our cabin and you'll find a bottle of whisky in the locker beneath the lower bunk. Bring it up here and we'll have a couple of quick ones before we start getting grub for everyone.'

He must have had more than a couple. When I returned from draining the bilges, pumping water up to the fresh water tank and topping up the fuel tank, the level of the whisky was well down the bottle.

After we had eaten I tried once more to bring up the subject of our unsatisfactory anchorage. John cut me short and I detected an angry gleam in his eyes. Leaving him in the cabin, I went back up on deck.

The yacht was pitching rather a lot and I could see spray hissing over rocks to windward. It was not quite dark and looking shorewards to the small beach, I could make out black high tide marks. It was only about half-tide on the ebb at the moment, but there were already large waves crashing over the rocks in to the cove. Although I was worried, I knew better than to say any more to John. All I could do was search through the lockers, find another anchor and put it out over the stern. We were now more secure, but I was still far from happy.

When I returned below John was stretched out on his bunk, snoring. The cabin reeked of whisky, but I dared not open the port-hole. Had I done so we would have been flooded in no time at all. Although I thought sleep would be out of the question with such a storm blowing outside, I must have dozed off within minutes of lying down on my bunk.

I woke with a frightened start. It was a couple of seconds before I realised what had woken me. Then I heard a harsh, grating sound beneath the keel and the yacht gave a sudden, sideways lurch.

I swung myself up the short ladder to the deck and as soon as I lifted the hatch cover I realised what had happened. Spray hit me full in the face — and it was spray from the rocks! The strength of the storm had caused the anchors to drag. One of them had snagged on some underwater obstacle and was holding us barely an arm's length away from the rocks.

Hurrying below, I set about awakening John. It was not easy. Eventually he sat up, bleary-eyed and stupid, not aware where he was, let alone what was happening.

'Quick, wake up, man. We're aground.'

I hurried back on deck, thinking to rouse Mr Hardcastle and his girlfriend. However, as I made my way aft, desperately holding on to anything within reach, he raised his head above the hatchway that led to the passenger cabin.

'We're aground,' I shouted above the wind which was now howling in full fury. No sooner had I got the words out than the anchor broke free and we surged forward.

With a tearing, splintering noise, the yacht wedged itself between two rocks.

'There's water coming in down below,' he shouted. 'We'll have to lower the dinghy. It's our only chance.'

The dinghy was fastened down at the stern of the yacht. It would take a few minutes to take off the covers and swing out the davit in order to get it into the sea. Mr Hardcastle signalled he was going below to prepare Miss Meredith for the ordeal that lay ahead.

John and I fought our way to the stern and while he swung out the davits, I unlashed the dinghy.

Eventually we had it ready and it was swinging wildly over the stern. A few more turns of the winching handle and it would be low enough to step into.

I cupped my hands and shouted to John, 'I'll go down and tell the others to come up.'

Even as I spoke the yacht shuddered and we heard the sound of splintering wood from the bow.

'Don't be a fool,' John screamed at me. He pointed to the dinghy. 'Look! Look at it. Do you think it will hold four people in a sea like this? We'll be lucky if it doesn't capsize with just the two of us. Come on, get in!'

At first I could not believe what he was suggesting and I stood staring at him stupidly. He took a hold of my arm and impatiently thrust me towards the dinghy.

'Come on! Get in quick, before it's too late.'

I realised he was serious about leaving the others behind and I looked at him in horror.

'What about them? What about the others?'

He cursed me. 'Let them drown. Hurry up — are you getting in, or aren't you?' I shook my head. I could not believe he would really try to save his own life at the expense of the others. 'Then get out of my way. I'm going.'

He pushed me and I slipped and fell. Scrambling to my feet I caught hold of his arm as he was about to climb on board the dinghy.

He lashed out at me with his foot and I fell again.

He was half in the dinghy now and I almost sobbed at my inability to stop him.

Then my glance fell upon the winching handle. It was similar in type to a motor car starting handle — and it was detachable.

Pulling it free, I swung it at John, hitting him in the ribs. Turning, he kicked out at me yet again. I staggered, but did not lose my balance.

Steadying myself, I struck out once more. This time the blow caught him on the side of his face.

He fell backwards, his arms flailing in a vain effort to arrest his fall, trying to find something to hold on to. His fingers grasped the only thing within reach. The pin that held one end of the dinghy to the lowering wires.

The pin came out and the front of the dinghy crashed down, throwing John in the water. A large wave was on its way in. It picked him up and flung him against the rocks. Horrified, I watched him turn a cartwheel in the turbulent water. Then he was gone, the swell taking him over the rocks into the sea beyond.

Meanwhile the dinghy, attached to one remaining lowering wire, spun around crazily, smashing itself to pieces against the stern of the yacht.

Mr Hardcastle came up on deck, one arm about the terror-stricken Miss Meredith. He looked around for John, but there was no time for long, involved explanations. I pointed over the side of the yacht and then to the rocks.

He looked at me in horrified disbelief, but already I was shouting in his ear, giving him instructions.

I made Janet Meredith lie down in the well of the yacht's cockpit, then went below to start the engine. It was a powerful one — and would need to be if my plan was to stand any chance of success. While I was doing this, Mr Hardcastle was cutting the anchors loose and freeing the remains of the dinghy. I waited until an extra large wave lifted the yacht, then thrust the gear lever into 'Hard Astern'.

For an agonising moment I thought I had failed. Then, with a groan of strained timbers, the yacht slid free of the rocks.

I never really thought we would make it. The bow was half filled with water and sinking lower every minute, while waves broke over the stern with a frightening force. But, in the end, it was a wave that carried us to safety.

I had aimed the yacht at the small beach on the shore side of the cove. As I heard shingle grate beneath the keel, yet another great wave lifted us and carried the yacht up the beach.

Wet, but alive, we leaped from the bow of the boat and struggled to safety.

*   *   *

John's body was recovered a week later. I had to attend the inquest and told them a brief story about him falling from the dinghy while we were trying to lower it. They did not ask very many questions. They all seemed far too intent on building his image as a hero.

I left the village soon afterwards. As an expression of gratitude for my part in the incident, Mr Hardcastle set me up in a little tobacconist shop in a town close to his own home.

But for all these years I have wondered what sort of an epitaph they had given to John Summers. Now I know, I don't feel so bad about it. The fact that it is not the truth doesn't really

58

matter. An epitaph is not meant to be strictly factual, is it?

After all, I would not be very happy if I thought they would inscribe 'Harry Baxter, Murderer' on my tombstone.

All Colours are Grey

Inside the large greenhouse situated at the far end of the prison governor's garden, two men crouched low in a corner. They were hidden from view by the foliage of a number of bushy tomato plants. Blue smoke drifted into the air above them as they passed a cigarette between them, keeping a wary eye on a warder in the garden outside. He, in his turn, was watching a line of men in drab prison uniform weeding between the rows of half-grown pea plants.

'What you in for?' The older man put the question to his companion as he carefully passed over the hand-rolled cigarette.

'Armed robbery — and you?'

'Well, the judge called it burglary. Really, it's because I'm allergic to a colour.'

The younger man's jaw dropped and he almost lost the cigarette from his sagging mouth. Recovering quickly, he passed it back to his companion.

'You're *what* to a colour?'

'Allergic. It means I don't like grey — and grey don't like me.'

The young man shook his head in bewilderment. 'I'm sorry, I just don't get it.'

The older man eased himself back on his haunches and prepared to tell his story to the fellow convict.

'Well, it's like this, see. When I was a kid I was

quite bright. I passed all the exams I sat for, so they sent me off to a grammar school. Well, my old man was always in and out of the nick and we didn't have very much money. Couldn't afford a school uniform, or anything like that. All I had to wear was a grey jacket and a pair of grey trousers. Stood out like a sore thumb, I did. The other kids used to take the mickey out of me something cruel.

'One day, one of 'em took things a bit too far and I went for him. He was a lot bigger than me, so I had to use something that would even things up. The nearest thing to hand was a chair and that's what I used. The result was that I split his head open, got myself expelled from school, and was hauled up in front of a Juvenile Court.'

The younger man made sympathetic noises as he took the diminishing cigarette gingerly from the fingers of his companion.

'Ah, but it didn't end there!' the older man continued. 'That was before the war. When that lark began I was called up and put in the Royal Navy. They trained me as a gunner, then sent me out on an old converted merchant ship — one of the Grey Funnel Line, as it happened.

'There we were steaming up the English Channel one grey winter morning when — bang! We took a torpedo amidships and the ship sank in a matter of minutes.

'I managed to get myself into a dinghy, but it was just my luck that it drifted the wrong way and ended up in occupied France. The result was that I was taken prisoner and spent the rest of the war looking at the grey uniforms of the

Germans who were guarding us in the prison camp.'

The younger man coughed and handed over what remained of the cigarette.

'Thanks. I'll just have this one puff, then you can finish it off . . . There you are. Now, where was I? Oh yes, the end of the war.'

'When I got demobbed I had a bit of a job settling down. Then I found a nice little number, as a barman in a pub called the Grey Horse, over Hackney way. I enjoyed that. I might have been there now if the landlord hadn't caught me with my hand in the till. He was fairly decent about it, though. Never told the law. But he gave me such a good hiding I could hardly see out of me eyes for a week.

'I did a bit of 'knocking' after that. You know, pinching a little bit here and a bit there. Trouble was, I got myself caught too many times. I just didn't have a good eye for a store detective. Some blokes can spot them a mile off, but not me. The last time, I got three months for pinching a pullover — a grey one. Three months for that! Still, there it was.

'That was when I decided it was time I left the small stuff behind and got into something big. I did it, too,' he added proudly.

The younger man balanced the remaining fragment of cigarette between finger and thumb and took a careful drag.

'Yes, all set up right it was. A fashion house. I got to know one of the young girls who worked in there. By splashing out a bit of money on her in the pub around the corner I learned all about the layout of the place. I even found out they left the key to the safe in one of the drawers in the office. It was a piece of cake. Mind you, I didn't hurry anything. I bided my time until one night this young girl told me they'd pulled off some big deal with someone from the Middle East who'd insisted on paying them in cash. She said there was more than fifty thousand quid sitting in the safe.

'Well, that was it! I couldn't let a chance like that slip by, could I? It's the sort of opportunity that comes along only once in a lifetime.

'I pulled the job that night and it went like a dream. I filled my pockets with money — and still there was more. I had to stuff some of it inside my shirt. I'd never seen so much money before.

'I put the key back in the drawer, so it would look like an inside job, then got out of the window at the back. Just as I was putting my foot to the ground, I trod on a cat. I couldn't see what colour it was, it being dark, but I bet it was grey. Anyway, the damned moggy squealed so loud I lost my grip and fell down into a pile of dustbins. It made so much noise I must have woken up half the town. It was just my luck that a copper happened to be passing the end of the alley at that very moment. He had a grip on my collar before I'd even got to my feet.

'It wasn't until I got to court the next day that I realised just why my luck had run out. The fashion house had a French name, 'Maison Gris'. It was the copper who nicked me who told me that in English it means 'The Grey House'.

Well, can't win 'em all, can you?'

The sound of the greenhouse door opening brought both convicts scrambling to their feet, but they were already too late.

A warder stood at the door. A new prison officer. Neither of the two men had met with him before. Hands on hips, he glowered at them.

'So this is how you spend your time, is it? Top trustees, too. And what's all this smoke in here? No, don't tell me the tomato plants have been overheating. I may have only just come to this prison, but I'm no greenhorn. The best thing the pair of you can do now is to get yourselves down to the Senior Warden's office. Tell him I sent you.'

The two prisoners edged past the warder and made their way out through the door. It was the older of the two who stopped and put the question to him, hesitantly.

'Er . . . Who shall we say sent us?'

'Don't whisper to me, man. Speak up. Tell him you've been caught loafing — by Prison Officer Grey.'

Customs Die Hard

'Oh my God!' The gasp of disbelief came from Audrey, who was reading the local newspaper.

I looked up from my magazine. The tone of my wife's voice told me that what she was reading must be more personal than a train crash, or yet another motorway accident.

'What is it?' I asked, sharply, when she showed no indication of explaining her outburst.

Audrey lowered the newspaper slowly to the floor beside her, an expression of horror on her face. 'It's Peter and Jane. There's been a terrible boating accident. His body has been recovered, but they haven't found her yet.'

'I can't believe it!' I was utterly aghast. 'Why, we were talking to them right here in this house, only last Saturday.'

'Well it's here, on the front page,' she said, holding the newspaper out to me.

I took it from her hand and scanned the front page. There, half-way down, I saw the heavy, black headline. 'HEIR TO TIMBER FORTUNE DIES IN YACHTING TRAGEDY.' Beneath it, in slightly smaller print, it stated, 'Sir Peter Tilby's Body Found. Fiancée still missing.'

I read through the remainder of the news item. It seemed the couple had set out in Peter's yacht on Sunday from the Pentic Creek Yacht Club. They must have been out for no more than three hours when a sudden mist rolled in off the sea, reducing visibility to no more than a few yards. Other boats from the club were all fortunate enough to be within hearing distance of the bell-buoy situated at the entrance to the Pentic Creek channel. The yachtsmen quickly made their way back to safety — but Peter and Jane were not among their number. Nobody became unduly worried about their safety until after dusk had fallen. It had been believed they had probably anchored somewhere until the fog lifted, but now the coastguard was notified. Nothing was discovered until Tuesday morning. It was then that pieces of wreckage, identified as being from his boat, were washed up on the rocky shore to the east of Pentic Creek. After a search of the area, Peter's body was recovered from the sea.

'They were so happy when we last spoke to them,' said a tearful Audrey. 'Jane was so delighted with the wonderful engagement ring Peter had bought for her. They were both full of the plans for their wedding. It's so dreadfully tragic.' Taking out a handkerchief, she blew her nose noisily. 'I've always said they should never have had a yacht club at that place. It's too dangerous. Mist and fog is always rolling in without warning — and the entrance to the creek is far too narrow.'

'You're right,' I agreed. 'It's the sixth boat lost there in the last three years.'

'Do you think we could find an excuse for not going down there this weekend?' sniffed Audrey, unhappily. 'I know Lord Quade's throwing a party, but I really don't feel like going to a party.'

'No, we must go,' I said, arriving at a sudden decision. 'It's his birthday and everyone will be there. For that very reason, I think I would like to go.'

Audrey gave me a quizzical look, but she knew me well. All she said was, 'All right, if you say so.'

We set off for Pentic Creek on Friday afternoon in perfect autumn weather, arriving late in the evening.

Pentic Creek is one of those delightful little Cornish corners, successfully defended by a maze of narrow, winding lanes. As a result, most holiday-makers very rarely find their way there. The creek also boasts a deep, tidal mud bank. This, and a total absence of sand, has enabled it to retain much of its original character. Nevertheless, the hotel and yacht club together have gained prominence in many of the books which extol the merits of such establishments. In the season it is extremely well patronised — by the yachting fraternity, in particular.

Many of the regulars were there when we arrived. Among them was Lord Trevor Quade, in the state of alcoholic benevolence that has made him such a popular host with his friends and many acquaintances over the years, much to the despair of his immediate family.

'Audrey, darling — and Caspar! So glad you could make it for my birthday. John, give them a double of their usual. No, I insist, darlings. Everything is on me, this weekend. My birthday present to you all for being such wonderful friends.'

We accepted our drinks from John, the

bearded, dark-visaged Cornish barman, and proposed a toast to our host's good health. He replied, from a distance, by waving his drink in the air in vague acknowledgement.

Audrey recognised someone she knew, who was currently one of London's top fashion models. As she made her way through the crowd to talk to her on her favourite subject — clothes — I saw Donald Ferguson, a particular friend of mine. Seated in a corner of the room, he had a beer in front of him and was nursing a faintly smoking pipe. When I went across to greet him, he moved along the bench to make room for me beside him.

After our initial greeting, I said, 'It's a nasty business about Peter. Has Jane's body been found yet?'

He nodded sadly, 'Yes, only this afternoon. She was caught up among the rocks along the coast about two miles from here. The body was in a bit of a state I believe, poor girl.'

'Where did they take her body?' I asked.

Donald gave me a puzzled look. 'To the mortuary at St Degan's. Is this idle curiosity, or professional interest?'

Choosing not to answer him, I said, 'If we were to sneak out of here for a while, do you think I could have a look at her?' Donald is the coroner for this particular district. As such, he carries a certain amount of judicial power.

'Of course, but . . . ' He stopped. Shrugging his shoulders, he said, 'I'll ask no more questions. My car will be outside the front door for you in five minutes. See you there.'

Pausing only to tell Audrey that I was leaving the club to have a look at Donald's new boat and would be back in about half an hour, I hurried outside. Audrey and the model were so engrossed in discussing the latest Paris collection, I doubt if she even heard a single word I said to her.

Because of Donald's position, we had no problem in gaining access to the mortuary and I braced myself as the long drawer containing the body was slid open on smooth metal runners.

She had certainly taken a battering from sea and rocks. The poor girl was barely recognisable. I remained looking at the body for no more than two minutes. Then Donald covered her over with a sheet and we went outside.

'Did you find what you were looking for?' Donald asked the question as he struck a match and held the flame to his pipe.

'Yes.'

I took a cigarette from my case in time for Donald to hold out his match. He dropped it quickly to the ground as it burned his fingertips.

'Are you out sailing tomorrow?' I asked, as we drove back to Pentic Creek.

'I was seriously thinking about it. Why do you ask?'

'I would like you to do something for me,' I said. 'Something important. Now, listen very carefully . . . '

When I had completed my explanation, Donald said, dubiously, 'I'll do it, of course, but I would like to know what this is all about.'

'Don't question anything,' I replied. 'Just do as

75

I ask and I'll explain everything to you tomorrow.'

Donald shrugged, 'I hope you have a *good* explanation but, all right, I'll do as you say. Now, here we are, back at the jolly party.'

When we walked inside the yacht club I don't believe anyone had even missed us. The party was beginning to warm up, so I thought I would do what needed to be done, before everyone became too drunk.

'Darling,' I said to Audrey, 'I'm afraid I need to return to town tomorrow, to complete some work. I'm terribly sorry, but it really is quite unavoidable.'

Audrey pouted. 'Oh, Caspar! Do you really *have* to? I have been so looking forward to this weekend.'

'There's no need for you to come back with me,' I said. 'I hope to be back sometime tomorrow night. I'm quite sure Lord Quade will be only too happy to take you out with him on his boat.' Lord Quade had a magnificent, if somewhat ramshackle yacht. Until recently, he had employed a crew of three to sail it for him. Now he was glad to have yacht club members go out with him as crew.

I called to him across the room. 'Trevor, I have to return to town on business tomorrow, but I would hate to spoil Audrey's weekend. Would you mind taking her with you for the day, if you're going out?' I needed to shout loudly in order to make myself heard above the buzz of conversation in the bar.

'Of course, old boy. It will be a pleasure,' he

76

shouted back. 'Tell the darling girl I'll be putting to sea at about ten o'clock. Dozens of the club are coming along too. I'll have a marvellous crew!'

I waved my thanks and turned back to Audrey. The model with whom she was talking had overheard the conversation between myself and Trevor and was enthusiastic at having Audrey's company on the yacht.

'Darling, how wonderful! We'll be able to have a lovely chat together,' she said as she spilled champagne from her glass over the carpet. 'I am so glad you're coming.'

At that moment I caught sight of Donald. He appeared to be having a little trouble at the bar and I hurried to his assistance. 'What seems to be the matter?'

Red-faced and angry, he waved a bulging wallet in the air. 'They won't let me pay for a damned drink,' he said.

'Of course they won't,' I explained, soothingly. 'Today is Lord Quade's birthday and he's in the chair. Nobody pays for a drink this weekend.'

Donald calmed down immediately. 'How silly of me. But here I am with over a thousand pounds in my wallet that I won on the horses — and I can't spend a penny of it!' Thrusting the wallet back inside his pocket, he grinned. 'Oh well, it will keep for another time.' He slapped me on the back and in a hearty voice said, 'Pity you're not able to go sailing tomorrow, Caspar. I intend going out to have a look at the Eddystone lighthouse. I would have liked to give you a race, there and back — for a small wager, of course.'

'I say, I wouldn't go that far out if I were you,' said one of the sailing crowd. 'It's not a very good weather forecast for tomorrow. A bit squally. It would probably be better if you just pottered about in the bay like the rest of us.'

'Nonsense!' declared Donald. 'I'm going to Eddystone. Mine is a good sea-boat and I'll be back not long after dark.'

The man who had given him the warning threw him a resigned look, then walked away to rejoin his friends without saying anything more.

The party did not break up until quite late that night and I left before most of them were awake, the next morning.

I was waiting on the jetty when Donald sailed into Fowey harbour at three o'clock that afternoon. Rain had been driving in off the Channel for a couple of hours and he was wet and decidedly disgruntled.

'Now, do you mind telling me what this is all about?' he asked, as we sat inside the sea-front restaurant. 'I must be mad, sailing all this way in such weather, for no other reason than that you wanted me to!'

'Have a little patience, Donald,' I said. 'You'll have your answer today — I hope — but you'll need to wait for a few hours more.'

His mood mellowed a little when the public houses in the town opened. In fact, a couple of brandies later he was his usual cheerful self.

We were still drinking when dusk fell and I thought it time we moved off. After driving westwards at a fast pace for an hour and a half, I turned off the main road. Here we were forced to slow down because of the narrow, winding lanes.

Soon, the headlights of the car illuminated a signpost which showed we were only three miles from Pentic Creek. I turned the car into the gateway of a nearby field. 'This is as far as we go in the car. It's an absolutely filthy night, so you'd better put your oilskin jacket back on. You'll find a spare torch in the glove compartment. Put it in your pocket — but on no account use it unless I say so.'

'Where the hell are we going?' asked Donald as we left the warmth of the car behind and turned off the road to climb over a wooden stile.

'You'll see, all in good time,' I replied. 'For now just keep quiet and follow me. I hope I can remember where to go. This morning was the first time I'd been along this way.'

We walked for twenty minutes before I spoke again. 'Watch your step now.' I whispered the cautionary words, 'Part of the path runs on the very edge of the cliff. One slip might prove fatal . . . Do you hear that?'

Far below us, away to the left there was the sound of surf, pounding the cliffs and pouring back over the rocks. We half-walked and half-scrambled for another ten minutes before I reached back to bring Donald to a halt.

'Listen! What do you hear?'

Donald stopped and then he too heard the distant tolling of a bell, rendered intermittent by the driving wind.

'It's the bell-buoy marking the entrance to the

Pentic Creek channel,' he replied.

'Is it?' I said, enigmatically, as I brushed the back of my hand across wet eyelashes. 'I think you're in for a surprise, Donald.'

The insistent, unrhythmical notes of the bell became louder as we scrambled on. Then I halted once more.

'Still hear it?' I asked, quietly.

'Of course,' replied Donald. 'It's . . . Good God!'

'Go to the top of the class,' I said grimly. 'It *sounds* like the Pentic Creek channel buoy, but Pentic Creek is a mile and a half away. That bell is directly below us. Somewhere among the rocks.'

'But . . . ' Donald's voice expressed his disbelief. 'No one would do a thing like that! It's . . . It's just not human!'

'That's as may be,' I replied. 'Nevertheless, it was once a recognised source of income for the more unscrupulous coastal dwellers — and customs die hard in these parts. Quietly now, we'll make our way down there.'

The sound of the bell grew louder as we made our way cautiously down the rough, winding path that led down to the rocks below.

We must have been some fifty feet from the base of the cliffs when I saw the light of a cigarette, cautiously held in a cupped hand, not ten yards ahead. Whoever was smoking it was crouched behind the shadow of a large rock, sheltering from the buffeting wind.

Before I could reach out to bring Donald to a halt, he stepped on a stone which rolled away from beneath his feet and he let out a startled oath.

The opportunity of taking the hidden man by surprise had gone. Pulling a torch from my jacket pocket, I pressed the switch. A thin, bright beam of light sliced through the night. The man with the cigarette was already on his feet and clambering along the side of the cliff, away from us.

I barely had time to take in the thin rope which stretched away down the slope towards the now silent bell when a scream of terror escaped the lips of the fleeing man.

In the light from my torch I saw him teeter on one leg at the edge of a sheer drop. Arms windmilling, he made a desperate attempt to regain his lost balance.

A gust of wind off the sea seemed to help him for a split second, then the wind dropped without warning. He dropped too, falling like a stone, his scream fading into nothingness.

Donald and I went down the path as quickly as caution would allow. We found the man spread-eagled on the rocks just above high-tide mark. He was quite dead.

'Recognise him?' I asked.

'Yes,' replied Donald, soberly. 'It's the son of the yacht club barman. He often helped out on the jetty.'

'That's right,' I agreed. 'Now the last piece of the puzzle has fallen into place. Come on, we've one last task to carry out tonight.'

★ ★ ★

81

Two uniformed policemen, an inspector and a sergeant, were waiting for us in the car park of the yacht club when we returned to Pentic Creek.

I spoke to them briefly before Donald and I entered the building together.

It was rather quiet and subdued in the bar when we pushed the door open but, when the occupants saw Donald they set up a shout that could have been heard a mile away.

'Donald! Where have you been? We've all been worried sick about you. We thought you must have still been out at sea. What have you been doing?'

'He's been out with me,' I said.

'What for? And how is it you're with him? You're supposed to be in town, on business!'

'I've been on business all right,' I said, 'But not in town. I've been investigating a long established and most unusual family business. Old-fashioned Cornish wreckers, no less.'

From the corner of my eye I saw the barman edge his way towards the door that led to the yard, at the back of the yacht club. Donald saw him too and caught hold of my arm to draw my attention to him.

'Leave him!' I snapped.

When his hand gripped the handle, the barman flung open the door — and ran headlong into the arms of the two policemen.

The light from the bar glinted briefly on polished steel, then the handcuffed barman was hurried away to a waiting police car.

'Is there anything else, Sir?' asked the

inspector, showing himself at the door.

'I think you have the main business well in hand,' I replied. 'But don't forget to search the rooms occupied by the barman and his late son. I think you'll find some articles of considerable value hidden there. Oh yes! Perhaps you would be kind enough to make arrangements for someone to remove whatever has been used to muffle the buoy marking the Pentic channel. I will be in touch with your Chief Constable again in the morning, but I have already given him most of the information about the case. Thank you, Inspector — and well done.'

The inspector saluted and went out, closing the door behind him.

'I suppose someone should inform the secretary that we'll require a new barman,' I said, as I helped myself to a large brandy and passed another, of equal size, to Donald.

'I still don't understand how you realised what was going on,' said Lord Quade, when I had finished telling the party of the day's events.

'It was mainly guesswork, with a little deduction thrown in,' I explained. 'There have been six 'accidents' in three years. All those who were killed when their boats were wrecked were fairly wealthy people. Most were likely to be carrying something of value with them. In poor Jane's case it was an engagement ring worth something close to twenty thousand pounds — but it was not on her finger when her body was found. I checked against the list of her personal effects, held in the mortuary.

'This was why I asked Donald to pretend to

have a thousand pounds in his pocket. It made it probable that whoever was responsible for wrecking the boats would make an attempt to get him when he was due to be the last boat in tonight. It needed to be the last boat, or they would not dare try anything. Had there been more than one boat involved and a survivor told of the false channel bell, the game would have been up right away.

'I think every one of us here realises just how simple the plan was. When conditions out there are bad, we head straight for the sound of the bell-buoy without even thinking about it. We know that once we pass it by we're almost home. If the real bell is muffled and another substituted, we all know what will happen. Crash! We're on the rocks — and there's someone waiting to ensure we don't get off alive.'

I looked around the hushed and horrified assembly.

'It's perhaps justice that it was poor Peter who set me on the right track. It was something he said to me the last time we met, in this very bar. He pointed to the wall above the fireplace and said, 'I wonder what happened to the picture they used to have up there? The one called 'The Wreckers'. It was a very good one. I'm surprised they decided to take it down.' '

I drew a cigarette from my case and lit it while the import of my words sunk in.

The silence in the room was broken by the nervous, shaky laugh of Lord Quade.

'Thank the Lord we have an Assistant

Commissioner in charge of CID among our members. I intend taking my yacht out to the Channel Islands tomorrow. I won't be returning until well after dark. I might well have been the next victim!'

I felt almost sorry for Lord Quade. He possessed little but his title and a yacht that would not survive another winter season. In fact, before leaving London I had been studying a file the Metropolitan Police had opened on him. He was known to have been making enquiries among some of the city's petty criminals, seeking a man who would set fire to his boat when his Lordship could be proved to be many miles away.

It was similar to the act committed by his father, who had set fire to the ancestral home, in a bid to claim on the substantial insurance taken out on the house.

Yes, indeed. It seemed that in this part of the world, customs *do* die hard.

A Very Fine Fiddler

Percy Tewkesbury is a violinist. Perhaps not one of the world's greatest, but good enough. Anyway, he earns his living that way. But if you've ever been one of the regular concert-goers at the Albert Hall you'll not need me to tell you that. You will have heard him for yourself. However, it was not his art that was worrying Percy that night I met him in the bar of The Wagoners — you know, the little pub in the side street, around the corner from the Albert Hall.

I noticed him as soon as I went in, even though he was sitting in the shadows just outside the log fire's glow. His rather frail body was hunched over the table and those long, sensitive fingers were curled around a pint tankard of best bitter. I've known Percy for a good many years, so I ordered my beer and had no hesitation in taking it across to his table and seating myself opposite him.

'Hello, Percy,' I said, breezily. 'What are you sitting over here all alone for?'

He looked up at me, misery showing in his eyes and just nodded his head. 'Oh, good evening, Eric.' Then he stared down into his beer and gave a deep sigh, his fingers playing abstractedly with the handle of the glass.

I was rather alarmed. Percy was usually pretty cheerful. I'd never before seen him so despondent.

'Now, come on Percy,' I said. 'This isn't like you. What's the matter?'

When he didn't answer I tried a bit of persuasion. 'You can tell me, surely?' I coaxed. 'After all, us musicians have to stick together you know.'

Yes, I forgot to mention it before, but I too am a violinist. I play in the second row of the North Acton Concert Orchestra.

Percy looked up at me then, indecision on his face. He stared at me for about a minute before making up his mind. Sinking the remainder of his beer, he put the glass down heavily and said, 'It's Mabel — or, to be more exact, her mother.'

I knew all about Mabel, of course. She was Percy's betrothed. The engagement had come as a great surprise to all of us. For all his — oh, fifty-odd years, he'd appeared to be that most perfect of beings. A confirmed bachelor. Then one night he'd brought Mabel into this very bar and introduced her as the lady he intended to marry! As I remember it, the celebration that followed the announcement was one of the best I have ever taken part in, but that is purely incidental.

'What's her mother got to do with things?' I asked with a smile. 'Won't she give you two her blessing?'

This was intended as a bit of a joke because Mabel had seen the age of consent come around twice, plus a few more years thrown in.

'You may laugh,' said Percy, 'but that's just the trouble. Mabel lived with her mother for years

90

and she's still very much under her thumb. She went home this weekend to tell the old lady about us getting married and it seems she went off the deep end. Said that a musician doesn't have a settled job and all that stuff, you know? Anyway, she's coming to London to see me play and I'm in a fix, especially now that the season's finished at the Albert Hall. I'm at my wits' end. Don't know what to do. One thing's certain though. If her mother's against the wedding, it's off. Mabel will do as she says.'

Calling for another beer, I nodded sympathetically. 'Hmm! Yes, I can see your problem,' I said. 'It's a bit difficult, isn't it?'

We talked about it for a couple more rounds and, well, you know how drink can affect some people. They become expansive. Friends with the world at large. Well, I'm like that. A few snorts and I'll give the earth to anyone I happen to be with at the time.

So it was that when the solution to Percy's little problem came to me in a blinding flash of inspiration, I didn't even stop to think.

'I've got it!' I shouted, so suddenly that I had to pause to thump Percy's back. A mouthful of beer had gone down the wrong way.

When he'd finished coughing and spluttering, I said excitedly, 'Look, Percy, I've got a great idea. When's the old lady coming?'

'Next week,' he said.

'Great!' I said. 'Couldn't be better. Now, you know that next week the North Acton Orchestra is giving a series of concerts in various parts of London?'

Percy didn't know, but he nodded politely anyway.

'Right,' I went on. 'Now, if I was to go sick at the last minute, just before one of the concerts started and I recommended you to take my place, do you think you could do it? I'd give you the music beforehand so you could get some practice in.'

His face was a picture. It glowed, and I saw him smile for the first time that evening.

'Could I do it?' he exclaimed. 'Just give me the chance, that's all I ask.'

He leaned over the table, grasping my hand in both of his. 'Would you do that for me, Eric? Would you really do that to help me?'

'Consider it done,' I said.

There were tears in Percy's eyes as he called for yet another drink and I felt the smug warmth that comes from helping a fellow man spreading deep inside me.

★   ★   ★

Everything went exactly as we had planned it. At first, that is.

The old girl arrived and I got complimentary tickets for the concert for her and Mabel. I waited until half an hour before the concert was due to begin before I telephoned the conductor to say that I'd been taken ill. At such short notice he was only too pleased to accept Percy as a replacement.

I could hardly wait for the next morning to find out how things had gone for him.

His voice on the telephone was jubilant. 'Marvellous,' he babbled. 'Absolutely marvellous. I can't thank you enough, Eric. Then he sobered down. 'There's just a little problem, though . . . '

'What is it?' I asked, concerned that Percy might not have come up to the North Acton's high musical standards. 'You didn't make a mess of that difficult passage in the scherzo, did you?'

'No,' replied Percy, 'the concert went off very well. That's partly the trouble. Mabel's mother enjoyed it so much that she wants to go again tonight.'

'Oh,' I said, with relief. 'Is that all? Well, that's all right. You just turn up again and tell the conductor I'm still sick.'

Percy was most effusive in his gratitude and promised to call me the next day.

I hadn't heard from Percy by lunchtime and when I rang his landlady, she told me he was out. I didn't worry. I knew I would see him around soon anyway.

That evening I dressed carefully and with my violin tucked beneath my arm, I caught the Underground to the hall where that night's concert was being held.

I was told I was not wanted.

The conductor was most apologetic. 'I'm sorry, Eric,' he said. 'But I didn't know when you'd be fit again and I couldn't afford to be a violinist short. I've taken on that man you recommended for the rest of the tour. He's very good, you know. I'm most grateful to you for recommending him to me. Now, if you'll excuse me, I have to run along. Come and see me some time, Eric. 'Bye for now.'

I was absolutely flabbergasted! After all, I had been playing for the North Acton for years.

I tried to see Percy after the concert, but Mabel and a hard-eyed old battle-axe, who I took to be Mabel's mother, were waiting for him and he didn't see me. At least, I don't think he did.

The next few months were rather lean ones for me. Violinists are not exactly in great demand. I was glad when the Albert Hall concert season began again and I was able to take Percy's place there.

He was on tour with the North Acton, somewhere on the Continent. I saw an article in the paper about it. It mentioned that the orchestra's recently promoted second violinist, Mr Percival Tewkesbury, was taking his new bride along, for a Continental honeymoon.

I saw them both about a month later, while I was playing at the Albert Hall. Arm in arm they were and, in spite of all I'd done for them, they didn't even stop to speak to me.

The two of them just stalked past, noses in the air, completely ignoring the cap on the pavement and me, standing in the gutter, playing my heart out to the concert queue.

The Gambler

'May we have a little silence, please! Mr O'Dwyer, do you hear me?'

The sound of knives and forks clattering on plates gradually died away. Reluctantly, Mr O'Dwyer cut short the story about the Englishman, the Scotsman and the Catholic Bishop with which he was regaling Mr Trelawney. As that gentleman was rather deaf, Mr O'Dwyer had been talking very loudly. The sudden interruption caused a certain amount of distress to Miss Daintey who was blushing in anticipation of the story's ending.

'Thank you, Mr O'Dwyer. I am quite sure Mr Trelawney will look forward to hearing the remainder of that story — in private!'

'Now,' Sister Dominique looked around the dining room of the Order of Charity's home for Senior Citizens, a typewritten sheet of paper in her hand. 'I am delighted to be able to tell you that I have here an invitation from Mr Goftopoulous for you to look over his new hotel.'

There was an immediate buzz of interest from the diners. Multi-millionaire Mr Goftopoulous had been much in the news recently, on account of the hotel he had built on the sea front. He claimed that within its confines the hotel had everything for which a family on holiday might wish. A ballroom, modern gambling casino, heated swimming-pool, bowls room, snooker room . . . The hotel had them all.

Sister Dominique held up her hand for silence. 'The invitation is for next Monday and Mr Goftopoulous himself will be there to show you around.'

The residents of the home resumed their meal amidst excited chatter. Mr O'Dwyer's voice boomed out, 'He's looking for custom — in case we ever decide to take a holiday.' His hearty laugh mingled with the throaty chuckle of Mr Trelawney.

'All the same,' Miss Daintey twittered, 'I'm quite sure it will be a very interesting day. Will you be going, Mr O'Dwyer?'

'That depends on whether anything more interesting comes along before then.' This was a joke and all three were aware of it. Invitations like this were few and far between for a trio like them, whose combined ages totalled two hundred and forty-one years.

★   ★   ★

On Monday afternoon the residents of the home were ready and waiting when two coaches, dazzling with their glass and chrome fittings, drew up at the the gate of the home. Six of the nuns were to accompany them and they circled around them like sheep-dogs in the driveway, coaxing here and scolding there as their charges boarded the vehicles.

The ride itself was a treat enough for many of the elderly men and women. They chattered like excited schoolchildren along the way, pointing out landmarks they had once known well and the newer building projects, and commenting on the fashions of the youngsters walking on the streets through which they passed. For others, the town held memories that were too close, too personal and often painful. They said nothing, hugging their thoughts silently within themselves.

When they reached the hotel, Mr Goftopoulous was waiting to greet them — and he was literally giving them red carpet treatment. The carpet stretched from the hotel entrance, down the steps and to the covered arch where the coaches stopped. After greeting each of them with a handshake, the hotel owner led the way inside the building.

It was the beginning of a memorable visit. A whole army of hotel employees had been detailed to attend to their every need throughout the afternoon. As Miss Daintey said, 'They're treating us just as though we were film stars!'

Mr O'Dwyer seemed to be taking it all in his stride, behaving as though he was accustomed to receiving such treatment. Only Mr O'Dwyer himself knew that he was so overawed he dared say nothing. Not even 'Thank you', for fear he might betray his feelings.

The guests took tea by the swimming-pool and were then taken to the ballroom where a band played old-time dance music for them. Those who did not want to listen were shown the snooker and bowls rooms.

At five o'clock, Mr Goftopoulous announced the grand climax to the day's visit.

When they were all gathered together, he

stood on a chair and made an announcement, his accent betraying his Mediterranean origins. 'Ladies and gentlemen. I will now show you my casino. It is the most modern in the country and my croupiers are the best in the whole world. As you enter you will be given five small yellow discs. Each of these represents a pound. You may cash them in immediately, if you wish. If not, I trust you will sample the thrill of gambling for yourselves.'

'How exciting!' exclaimed little Miss Daintey. Her words were echoed by most of the others. There was hardly one of them who did not spend an ill-afforded percentage of his, or her, pocket-money on a weekly flutter on the lottery.

The casino was a large and magnificent room, high domed, with a plush carpet and dimly lit except for bright lights above each green baize table. For this occasion, only one table was actually in operation — the roulette table. The residents of the retirement home crowded around and began cautiously placing their bets. There were more groans than cheers as they risked their pound tokens.

Mr O'Dwyer watched the game for a few minutes to discover what it was all about. He arrived at the conclusion that this was very much like the football pools — something that only other people won. By the time he had edged close enough to the table to take part in the game, he had made up his mind what he would do.

Taking all five of his chips, he made a small pile of them on number thirteen. The others placed their bets, the roulette was spun and the ball tossed in. It free-wheeled around the rim of the wheel until it came to rest in one of the many slots.

As the wheel slowed down, the winning number was called.

'Lucky number thirteen!'

There was a gasp from the others around the table as piles of chips were placed on the table and pushed across to Mr O'Dwyer. Even he was impressed. 'How much do I have here?' he asked the croupier.

'One hundred and eighty pounds, Sir. You put on five pounds and it paid thirty-five to one.'

A strange light came into Mr O'Dwyer's eyes. An experienced observer would have recognised it as 'gambling fever'.

'That's a good start,' he said. 'Now, what number shall I have next? I know, my birthday. That's the twenty-first.'

There was a gasp from those watching as he pushed the whole pile of chips across the table to number twenty-one.

'Any more bets, please?'

The others were reluctant to bet. They preferred, instead, to watch Mr O'Dwyer's grand fling. The wheel was spun, the little steel ball dropped in and there was silence until the ball dropped into a slot.

In the same professional voice as before, the croupier announced, 'Number twenty-one.'

There was a roar of delight from the crowd which now included a number of hotel employees who had heard what was happening.

This time it was a great pile of multi-coloured chips pushed across the table to Mr O'Dwyer, who said, 'How much have I got now?'

'Six thousand, four hundred and eighty pounds, Sir.'

'Six thousand, four hundred and eighty pounds!' The amount was repeated among the onlookers and now everyone tried to get close enough to congratulate Mr O'Dwyer.

'You're rich!' cried Mr Trelawney, pummelling his friend on the back. Even the thin-lipped Sister Dominique managed a smile. Mr O'Dwyer did not appear to be listening. His face pale, he stared at the great pile of chips on the table in front of him. There was a sudden hush as it dawned on the others what he was contemplating.

'No! Mr O'Dwyer . . . you can't even think of it. What if you lose it all?'

A very agitated Miss Daintey was plucking at his sleeve and Sister Dominique began pushing her way through the crowd, a grim expression on her face. 'Mr O'Dwyer . . . '

She was too late. By the time she reached him he had pushed all the chips forward.

'We'll have Miss Daintey's birthday now. Put it all on number eight.'

'But, Mr O'Dwyer . . . ' Miss Daintey was close to tears.

'Shhh!' Mr O'Dwyer patted her arm.

Above the heads of the crowd, the croupier caught the eye of Mr Goftopoulous. Immediately, he called, 'Any more bets, please?'

All was silence, except for the metal ball

bouncing around the edge of the wheel. When it stopped, everyone craned their heads forward, attempting to discover for themselves what number it occupied.

'Number . . . nine.'

There was a loud groan and the croupier gathered all of Mr O'Dwyer's chips in the kitty.

Moments later the gambling recommenced, with the residents of the home playing their pound chips once more. The excitement had left the table and only Mr O'Dwyer appeared unconcerned by his loss. His attitude infuriated Sister Dominique. 'Mr O'Dwyer! Do you realise what you have just done? You have thrown away almost six and a half thousand pounds. It's a foolish old man you are, to be sure!'

Mr O'Dwyer looked at her and frowned. 'Sister, what's the first thing a man has to prove before he can be admitted to the Order of Charity's home?'

Sister Dominique was somewhat nonplussed, 'Why . . . you have to prove you are destitute, but . . . '

'And if I had more than six thousand pounds I would have to leave, would I not?'

'Well . . . '

'Thank you. I don't think six and a half thousand pounds would be enough for me to find somewhere else to live and keep myself for the remainder of my life. It certainly wouldn't buy the many friends I have at the home. No, Sister, I am not such a foolish old man.'

'Well said!'

Mr Goftopoulous had been an interested

eavesdropper. Now he came forward and took Mr O'Dwyer by the hand, shaking it vigorously.

'It is a pleasure to meet such a gallant loser,' he said. 'I wish everyone who lost money in one of my casinos behaved in such a way.'

Still holding Mr O'Dwyer's hand, he beamed at him, 'Mr O'Dwyer, is it? I am so impressed that I am going to make a gift to you of a hundred pounds. No — please do not argue. Had you walked away when you were winning I would have been far more out of pocket. I want you to accept this hundred pounds and use it to give a party for all your good friends at the home. How does that appeal to you?'

Mr O'Dwyer accepted the notes held out by the hotel owner and murmured his thanks.

At that moment, Sister Dominique called, 'Time to be leaving, everyone. Please make your way to the coaches.'

* * *

Mr O'Dwyer sank back into the comfortable seat on board the coach with a sigh of relief. Miss Daintey was seated beside him. Mr Trelawney, a piece of paper in his hand, leaned across the gangway to speak to him.

'I've just been working out how much you would have won if number eight had come up.' Looking at the paper in his hand, he said with awe in his voice, 'It would have been getting on for a quarter of a million pounds. An absolute fortune.'

'A quarter of a million pounds, eh?' repeated

Mr O'Dwyer, quietly. 'Now that's a sum of money worth thinking about. Never mind, we didn't win.'

He turned to Miss Daintey and smiled. 'I'm afraid your birthday date didn't turn out to be a lucky number, Miss Daintey.'

'But that was what I was trying to say to you when you put all that money on number eight. My birthday is not the eighth but the ninth — and number nine won!'

Resume Normal Duties

At eight fifteen p.m. on a blustery late-summer evening, the pilot of the giant white bomber, homeward bound from a training flight over the North Sea, switched to the number two fuel tanks.

At eight sixteen p.m. the multi-million pound aircraft was plummeting down through the dark clouds. As it plunged seawards, strips of sheet metal peeled away from the starboard wing, twisted and buckled by an explosion in the outboard engine.

There had been no time to send out a distress call — and no need for the pilot to scream through the intercom for the crew to bale out and abandon the stricken aircraft. From explosion to burial in the deep, grey waters far below took less than four minutes. But the sun was a quarter of an orange, sinking beneath the heaving horizon, before the tragedy became known to the world.

A deep-sea trawler, homeward bound and gunwale deep with the harvest of a near-record catch almost missed the aircraft's survivors. Indeed, it might have run them down had not a sharp-eyed crew member seen them at the last moment. Reversing engines, the boat came to a pulsating stop not ten yards from where the RAF pilot and navigator bobbed in the water, linked by a thin white nylon cord.

Captain McKeown, of Her Majesty's Survey vessel *Livingstone*, had at that precise moment settled down in his cabin. A gin and tonic stood on the locker beside him and he held a month-old magazine in his hand.

Immediately below his cabin was the wireless office. The telegraphist on duty had just transmitted the anchoring position of *H.M.S. Livingstone*. He was contemplating writing a letter home when a loudspeaker in the corner of the office crackled into life. The loudspeaker was plugged into a receiver kept permanently tuned-in to the emergency frequency. It was a mere formality. Necessary only in order to comply with Service regulations. Nothing had ever been received on this particular frequency — until now! It was a couple of seconds before the telegraphist realised the source of the signal. When he did, he dived for the receiver, which was slightly off-tune. He twitched the dial until the message became clear.

' . . . Picked up two survivors from crashed aircraft in position 55.25 North, 01.38 East. Survivors state all crew should have escaped, with possible exception of Electronics Engineer. All ships in area please assist. Message ends.'

Hurriedly, the telegraphist compared the position with the anchoring signal he had recently despatched. The comparison was close enough for him to jab the buzzer to the Captain's cabin, and keep his finger held there.

'Captain here.' The voice echoed from the highly polished speaking-tube.

110

The telegraphist repeated the distress message. 'I've checked with our anchoring position, Sir. At a rough estimate I should say we're about eighty miles away.' The telegraphist kept excitement from his voice with the greatest difficulty.

'Good man!' There was only the slightest hesitation as the Captain's thoughts travelled ahead of him. 'Contact the ship that sent the message. Say we are on our way. I'll give an estimated time of arrival later. Copy the signal to the Commander-in-Chief.'

The insistent bells ringing between the bridge and the engine-room echoed faintly through the mess-decks of the survey vessel. Seamen and stokers cast puzzled glances at each other. The ship was at anchor!

The tannoy hummed its preliminary warning throughout the ship, followed by the voice of the coxwain. 'Duty watch close-up. Duty watch close-up. Prepare the ship to get under way.'

The surprised members of the crew jumped up from stools and swung out of bunks, pulling on jerseys and trousers and hopping into sea-boots. All wondered what had happened to disrupt the humdrum routine of a survey ship.

They were not kept in suspense for long. As the first men reached their places of duty, the Captain spoke to them, his voice loud and metallic through the speakers.

In a few terse phrases, he told them of the signal and of the drama being played out eighty miles away, in a sea that was becoming rough.

'I would like to remind the men detailed as

look-outs of their responsibility. The lives of a number of men depends upon their vigilance. Men who are not as well equipped as we are to survive on the sea and who may be handicapped by burns, or other injuries. This is a rescue operation. I expect every man on this ship to do all within his power to ensure its success.'

The anchor slowly came up through the deep, green waters, the chain clattering noisily into the huge, cylindrical locker situated just forwards of the seamen's mess-deck. Moments later, *H.M.S. Livingstone* steamed eastward into the dusk.

Very few members of the ship's crew were able to sleep that night. The Captain crouched on his stool on the bridge, surrounded by officers, signalmen and seamen look-outs. Below, on the deck, off-duty sailors propped themselves up in sheltered nooks and crannies and stared out into the night. Each man hoped he might be the first to sight the bobbing red light of a life-jacket that would mean rescue for one of the airmen. Below, in the wireless office, all three of the ship's telegraphists were on watch. They had taken on the self-imposed task of radio control as first one . . . two, then more ships joined in the search.

When dawn broke, grey and damp around the bleary-eyed sailors on deck, there were eleven ships scouring the heaving seas. All were seeking five airmen who had been at the cold mercy of the sea for almost twelve hours. Daylight brought fresh hope to the searchers. It also widened the horizons of the search area. The sea was reduced to squares on a map, each square allocated to a ship and ticked off when it had been thoroughly scoured.

At midday, the RAF pilot and navigator were transferred from the trawler to the survey ship. The sailors, gathered at the top of the gangway with the intention of giving them a warm welcome, fell silent when they saw the grief and anguish painted on the strained face of the pilot. Like many of the greatest men who had enlisted in the service of his hosts, he had lost his command. Yet the hardest part to bear was that although he was safe, the fate of his crew was uncertain — and hope was dwindling with every hour that passed. The two airmen were hurried away to the wardroom and *Livingstone* got under way once more, resuming the monotonous criss-crossing of her tiny patch of the North Sea.

It was a small Swedish coaster who first broke the bleak monotony of the day. Their Captain's voice boomed forth from the radio speaker situated on the bridge of the survey vessel.

'I think we can see something. Is a man in life-jacket. I am lowering a boat.'

During the ensuing silence there was an air of excited expectation on the bridge of *H.M.S. Livingstone*. They waited for the Swedish Captain to make a further report.

It came some ten minutes later. This time the voice was flat and void of emotion.

''Ello. It was one of the airmen we find. He is dead. Will you please to rendezvous with me. I will pass the body to you.'

It was while *Livingstone* was heading towards the Swedish coaster that one of the look-outs called Captain McKeown's attention to the antics of four or five gulls. They were circling and swooping low in an area some six hundred yards from the ship.

Captain McKeown immediately ordered the survey ship to head directly for the birds.

As they approached, the men on the survey ship could see the figure in the water. His yellow life-jacket bobbed up and down with the airman's head lolling back upon it.

'Lower the boat.' The Captain leaned over the edge of the bridge and gave the order to the sailors who waited beside a survey launch, already swung out over the ship's side.

The crew scrambled on board and no time was lost in lowering the launch into the water. As it set off from the ship and headed towards the man in the water, one of the gulls swooped to within inches of the face that was turned away from the ship.

'Hurry up!' Captain McKeown's voice boomed out through a loud-hailer. 'Quickly — before those gulls attack.'

The survey ship was drifting closer to the figure in the water now. It was possible to see the movement of the airman's arms. Whether it was a tired attempt at propulsion, or merely the movement of the sea, it was impossible to tell.

Those on board the ship were still not certain, even when they saw the limp figure of the airman dragged on board the launch. It was not until the launch came alongside the mother ship that the word went around.

'He's dead!'

Ironically, now it seemed to no longer matter,

114

the sea appeared anxious to give up her victims. By nightfall four flag-shrouded bodies were laid out on the quarter deck of *H.M.S. Livingstone.* They awaited the arrival of an RAF air/sea rescue launch that was on its way to convey them to shore.

After dinner, the officers sat quietly in the ship's wardroom. There was very little anyone wanted to say. The pilot of the crashed aircraft sat nursing a glass of brandy. He gazed into it as though it was a magic crystal ball that might blot out memories of the past and show only a picture of the future.

Captain McKeown made a brave attempt to inject some cheerfulness into the atmosphere.

'You can be quite certain we shall carry on searching, in the hope that the last remaining man of your crew is out there somewhere, alive and well.'

His words did not have the desired effect upon the airmen.

'I am sorry to have to say it, Captain,' said the pilot, 'but I think you will be wasting your time. The electronics engineer would not have had much of a chance. In order to escape he would have had to squeeze out of his cubby-hole and work his way forward through the aircraft, passing through the area where the fire was fiercest.'

The navigator agreed, 'He's right, Sir. It's not the easiest of places to get out of, even when the aircraft is on the ground.'

Captain McKeown appeared to be the only man who had not given up hope. 'Nevertheless, we will carry on searching and hope for the best.'

The air/sea rescue launch reached the survey ship shortly before nightfall. The crew of the naval vessel assembled in silent ranks upon the upper deck as the bodies of the airmen were piped on board the RAF craft. The pilot and navigator followed. Then, with a roar of powerful engines, the rescue boat pulled away, heading inshore. The rescued airmen paused to wave only once before they went down below to the comfort of the boat's cabin.

Captain McKeown looked about him at the officers and men who waited for him to tell them what they should do now.

'All right, what are we waiting for? There is still one airman unaccounted for. We'll continue the search.'

The scouring of the sea was resumed, but the 'life or death' atmosphere had gone. The wardroom stewards had overheard the pilot's remarks concerning the chances of finding the electronics engineer alive. Exercising their age-old prerogative as purveyors of wardroom gossip, they passed on their knowledge.

It seemed the other ships engaged in the rescue operation agreed with the pilot. The trawler which had been first on the scene was also the first to leave. The skipper radioed that he was low on fuel and unable to maintain the search any longer. During the night three other ships gave up the weary quest. Their reasons were less urgent, but painfully honest. They did not believe the last remaining member of the crashed aircraft's crew would be found. By noon of the following day only *H.M.S. Livingstone* was still in the area.

The Commander-in-Chief's thoughts were made apparent in a signal to the survey ship. 'In view of pilot's opinion and current lack of success, do you consider it worthwhile to continue the search?'

Captain McKeown's reply was abrupt to the point of rudeness.

'Yes.'

He gave no reason, and was not required to provide one. He was the Captain of his ship and sufficiently senior to exercise his power of command without question.

That night was cold and unseasonable. The wind was keen and a steady drizzle soaked through trousers and trickled inside the collars of the oilskins worn by the look-outs. Seamen grumbled as they were shaken from the warmth of hammocks to clatter up steel ladders and stand a cold watch on the upper deck.

'Cor! You'd never think it was still summer,' said the signalman on duty on the bridge, as he blew warm air into cupped, chilled hands. 'It's all right for the old man. He's got a nice warm cabin down below. Why doesn't he call the whole thing off before we all catch our death of cold?'

'The Captain's only just gone below,' retorted the coxwain. 'He'll be up here again before the hour's out, you mark my words. Anyway, you're not nearly as cold as that poor devil who's out there somewhere.'

The signalman snorted derisively, 'If he's out

there, you mean. If you ask me we're just wasting our time.'

'The Captain's not a man to waste time. His, or anyone else's. Just button your lip and keep a look-out. That's what you're up here for.'

Sniffing noisily, the signalman turned his back upon the coxwain. As he stared gloomily into the darkness, he shrugged the damp collar of his oilskin farther up his neck.

In his cabin, Captain McKeown lay on his bunk, fully clothed. The only light in the cabin was the faint red glow from his cigarette as he drew smoke deep inside his lungs and blew it out through pursed lips.

He was trying to make an appraisal — an honest appraisal — of the chances of finding the missing airman alive. It was not an easy decision to make. Against his decision to continue the search there was the testimony of the pilot and navigator of the crashed aircraft. That and the deteriorating weather and the bodies they had already recovered. Then he thought of the arguments in favour of carrying on — and it was here that doubt began. Was he really remaining in the area because he believed the airman was still alive? Or was the truth something more personal? A nagging memory he had tried to lock the door against, many years before?

A few months before the war ended, he had been a young lieutenant, in command of a small minesweeper. They had been on their way back to Rosyth, scheduled to arrive on the day his first child was due to be born. Then, as had happened on this occasion, a wireless message had caused a rapid change of plans. A trawler had struck a mine and sunk. His minesweeper was ordered to the scene. For three fruitless days they searched, while in a hospital in Rosyth doctors fought for the life of McKeown's wife. She had been rushed to the operating theatre, desperately ill following complications in the birth of their first child. No blame had been placed upon McKeown for giving up that search. Indeed, when an inquest was held upon the frozen bodies discovered in a life boat, some two weeks later, expert evidence was given that they had probably died within twenty-four hours of the trawler sinking . . . probably!

Captain McKeown sat up, ground his cigarette into a copper ashtray and made his way back to the bridge. There was no need to make an immediate decision. It could wait until dawn, at least.

By morning the drizzle had cleared. The sun climbed over the horizon in a blaze of pink and orange. On the bridge of the survey vessel, the Captain sat on his stool, his head gently dropping until the unshaven chin rested upon the top peg of the naval issue duffle-coat.

Suddenly . . . 'Something over there, Sir. On the starboard side. See . . . ? That patch of yellow.'

Startled to wakefulness, McKeown turned to look out over the water, squinting into the rising sun.

Suddenly he saw the object of the signalman's excitement. Rising on the crest of a wave, within moments it had slid down out of sight into the trough.

It was a dinghy!

'Wheel hard a' starboard, steer into the sun, coxwain. There's a dinghy out there.'

He tried to still the hope that rose inside him as the survey ship came closer to the bobbing rubber boat. It was not possible to tell whether there was anyone inside the dinghy. It had a waterproof canopy, rather like a small tent, rigged over it. The ship slowed as the dinghy bobbed nearer, but still there was no sign of life. Then a foam-capped wave lifted the rubber craft and spun it around — and there was the missing airman! Grey-faced and sick, he raised one hand in a weak salute. He was alive!

McKeown watched as a boat was lowered and went alongside the dinghy. The airman was gently lifted from his tiny wet and fragile rubber boat and brought to *H.M.S. Livingstone.*

As the airman was being helped on board the survey vessel, a signalman handed a wireless message to the *Livingstone's* commanding officer. Captain McKeown read it, then looked over the side of the bridge at the exhausted but ecstatic airman, now surrounded by a crowd of jubilant sailors. He closed his eyes as though in pain and screwed up the message he held in his hand, the words indelibly written on his mind: 'To *H.M.S. Livingstone* from Commander-in-Chief. Consider it a waste of time to continue search. Resume normal duties.'

Supper for One

Tucking the newspaper-wrapped package of fish and chips beneath his arm, Elijah Fink observed that the fat was beginning to seep through the wrapping. He carefully licked his fingers before exploring his pockets for the door key.

Elijah was a careful man.

He had to be, his freedom depended upon it. Receivers of stolen property trod a delicate line between police and villains, and Elijah Fink was one of the best fences in the business. Not as big as some of the West End fences, perhaps, but he had been in the business before most of them were born. Yet the only record on him in the police files read, 'Elijah Fink, 13th May, 1949. Bethnal Green Magistrates' Court. Riding a bicycle without lights. Fined ten shillings.'

He had inserted the key in the door of the dingy second-hand shop and turned it before he became aware of someone standing behind him. Turning quickly, he looked up into a rugged, broken-nosed face.

'Sorry, Mister,' said Elijah. 'I'm closed. Come back tomorrow.'

Pushing open the door, he scuttled inside the shop. The big man went in with him.

'My turn to be sorry, Mr Fink,' he said. 'The boss wants a word with you — and it won't wait.'

A large car glided to a halt outside the shop. Two men alighted and they too entered the shop.

Elijah recognised one of them immediately. He had once done business with Hatchet O'Keefe. That had been many years before. These days, Hatchet took his business to fences in the more prosperous part of London.

'Hello, Elijah,' said Hatchet, looking around the dingy shop. 'Things don't change very much around here, do they?'

The old man shrugged, 'Why should they? I make a living.'

'I know you do — but not from selling this rubbish.' Hatchet's gaze went around the shop before he inclined his head towards the stairs at the rear of the shop. 'Get up there, I want to talk to you.'

'What's the big idea?' Elijah protested as the broken-nosed henchman bundled him upstairs into the combined living-room and kitchen. 'I've done nothing to upset you.'

Elijah was pushed down in a sagging armchair and Hatchet flicked the corner of the table distastefully with his handkerchief before sitting down upon it to face him.

'Of course you haven't,' he agreed. 'And I sincerely hope you aren't going to, either.'

Elijah took the greasy package from beneath his arms. 'Is this going to take long? I've got my supper in here. I don't want it to get cold.'

'Anything to oblige.' Hatchet took the fish and chips from him and threw the package to one of his men. Wiping the grease from his hand with a handkerchief, he said, 'Put it in the oven for him, Archie.'

'And make sure you put the gas on low,' Elijah

called, as Archie opened the oven door.

There was a click from a cigarette lighter, the gas popped into life and Archie closed the oven door.

'Now,' said Hatchet. 'Let's get down to business, shall we? Where's the stuff that Geli-boy Flynn left with you?'

Elijah's face registered surprise. 'What stuff? I don't know what you're talking about.'

Hatchet leaned forward and glowered down at the old man. 'I don't want any of your lies, Elijah. You're Geli-boy's fence. He did a jewellers on Saturday. Got away with more than fifty thousand quid's worth, according to the papers. You see, Geli-boy lost a lot of money at a little gambling-place I own. He couldn't pay up, so I'm taking this stuff instead.'

'I've told you, I don't know anything about it,' protested Elijah. 'Why don't you ask Geli-boy where it is?'

'I can't,' retorted Hatchet, rising to his feet. 'He fell off a bus this morning and broke his neck. He's dead.'

Elijah began making sympathetic noises, but Hatchet cut him short with an impatient gesture of his hand.

'Forget it! I can see you're not going to be helpful.'

Speaking to his companions, he said, 'Turn the place over — and don't worry about making a mess.'

He held out a hand towards Elijah. 'I'll take the key to your safe.'

Elijah handed the key over without a protest

and the search began.

Hatchet's men made a thorough job of it. Drawers were pulled out and their contents strewn across the floor; vases were smashed and cushions torn open. They even ripped the back off the television set.

'A fine load of old rubbish you've got in there,' said Hatchet, handing back the key after examining the contents of the safe. 'I wouldn't give you a fiver for the lot.'

'That's right, you wouldn't,' retorted the old man. 'Not before I'd had the note checked at the bank, you wouldn't.'

'Very funny!' Hatchet raised his fist but violence was averted by the return to the room of his two men.

'There's nothing here anywhere, boss,' said one of them. 'Geli-boy must have hidden it somewhere else and not had time to pick it up.'

Hatchet glared at Elijah, then shrugged his shoulders. 'In that case there's no sense in wasting any more of our time here.'

Taking out his handkerchief once more, he dabbed at his nose. 'Come on, let's go. I can't stand the smell of this place any longer.'

One of the men grinned. 'That's your fish and chips, Elijah. I reckon you're going to have a burnt supper tonight.'

Elijah followed the three men to the front door of the shop and saw them off the premises. When they had gone, he pushed the heavy bolts into place and pulled down the blinds before returning upstairs to his flat. Switching off the oven, he reached inside and drew out the

126

package. Hatchet's accomplice had been right. The paper was scorched and brown. Placing it upon the table, Elijah unwrapped it carefully. There were very few chips and the piece of fish would not have made a meal for a kitten. The bulk of the package consisted of something wrapped inside a plastic bag. When he untied it, the contents spilled out across the table, twinkling and glittering in the light from the electric bulb.

'Well, well!' mused Elijah. 'Fifty thousand quid's worth, eh? Now it's all mine — except for a small percentage for Elsie Burt at the fish shop. She'll be able to take her daughter abroad for a nice holiday this year. I mustn't give her too much, though. It might start her talking. That wouldn't be good for business.'

Elijah Fink is a very careful and crafty old man.

Health and Beauty

'Oh, would we hae the giftie gie us, to see ourselves as others see us!'

Looking at his wife, Ethel, Arthur Gregory misquoted the hackneyed words of Robert Burns.

She sat hunched forward on the edge of the settee, her eyes riveted on the television screen, squinting now and then as smoke from the cigarette stub between her lips spiralled upwards. The smoke first touched her eyes, then the lock of colourless hair that protruded from beneath the square of faded silk she wore tied about her head in a bid to conceal a mechanical army of curlers.

'Blimey!' he groaned. 'To think I married her of me own free will. I must have been a nutcase.'

Ethel turned her head to look at him. Removing the damp cigarette stub from her mouth, she threw it sideways into the cinder-littered fireplace. As she did so, she grinned. It was a very hit-and-miss affair.

'Wot's the matter, luv? Got a 'eadache, 'ave we? Never mind, 'elp yourself to a swig of me beer and take a couple of aspirins. You'll find 'em in me 'andbag — if you can see it anywhere.'

Albert's blood temperature passed boiling point.

'It's not a headache I'm suffering from, it's *you*. Have you looked at yourself in a mirror

131

lately? You're a bleedin' mess, that's what you are. You've got no pride in your appearance.'

Looking around him wildly, he saw the small mirror hanging on the wall. It was decorated with a gaudy painting depicting an English country garden in one corner and the droppings of the budgerigar — whose favourite perch it was — in another. Snatching it from the wall, he thrust it in front of her face.

'Look at yourself. Just look! Have you ever seen such a mess in all your life, eh? Go on, tell me. Have you?'

Ethel, although offended, obligingly looked at herself in the smeared and dirty mirror. Putting her head to one side, she pushed back the lock of hair that had escaped the restraining clutches of both curler and headscarf.

'Why, wot's wrong wiv me? We ain't going nowhere, are we?'

Arthur tossed the mirror on the settee in disgust. 'Ain't going nowhere!' he mimicked. 'You're dead right we ain't going anywhere. What do you have to keep those things in your hair for, anyway?'

He waved a hand airily, 'All right, all right, I know. It's so your hair will look nice if we go out together. That's what you say, don't you? Well, what happened when I took you down to the pub last Thursday? 'I won't take me curlers out,' you said. 'Not worth it,' you said. 'I'll just change me headscarf and I'll be with you.' Blimey, woman, do you know you haven't had those things out of your hair for more than a month? Being in bed with you is like trying to get to sleep in a scrap-yard!'

This statement set Arthur off on another train of thought. 'That's another thing. You sit in front of that telly for so long that if it wasn't for the commercials you'd have rigger mertis set in. Oh, you needn't snigger like that. You're not the only one who watches the medical programmes.'

He sniffed and wiped the back of a hand across his nose. 'What good does all that watching do for you, that's what I'd like to know? Some poncey actor comes on and you go all gooey, imagining you're a teenager again. Then, when they get to the romantic bits you behave like some starry-eyed tart. Until we go to bed, that is. Then it's, 'No! Stop it, Arthur. I don't feel like it tonight.' Or, 'You can pack that up. If that's the sort of idea you pick up down at the pub you can stop going.' Yet who'd be the first one to break her heart if I ran off with some girl, eh?'

He gave a short laugh. 'That's a joke! I don't suppose you'd even notice I'd gone unless the telly broke down — and with some of the rubbish they have on there you probably wouldn't even know that had happened for a week or so.'

One of Ethel's favourite television series had just begun and she was not listening to him. 'Sh! Don't talk so loud, luv. Pass me the fags, will yer? They bounced off the settee when you threw the mirror down. I think they're under the table.'

Giving her a scathing look, Arthur kneeled down and groped beneath the table for the cigarettes. When he rose to his feet a dusty piece

133

of bacon rind was clinging to one knee of his trousers. Brushing it away, he threw the packet of cigarettes on Ethel's lap.

Without shifting her gaze from the small screen she located them and extracted a cigarette. Then she found the box of matches resting on the arm of the chair, alongside her. After three attempts, twice discarding dead matches that had been replaced in the matchbox, she succeeded in lighting the cigarette. The television programme had arrived at a gripping moment, with the heroine about to undergo a meaningful experience. The flame from the match reached Ethel's fingers and, wincing, she shook the black, curling sliver of charred wood to the floor.

Arthur watched this mute performance with undisguised contempt.

'Gor blimey!' he shook his head in mock disbelief. 'You ought to see yourself, Ethel. If that bleedin' goggle-box was a two way thing there would be no acting at the other end, I'm telling you. They'd spend all their time looking out at people like you. That's if there *are* any more quite like you.'

Ethel took in a lungful of smoke and coughed, waving blue smoke away from her face.

Arthur looked around him, an expression of distaste upon his face. 'Squalor, that's what this is. Squalor. A hovel — that's the word I've been trying to think of. We're living in squalor, in a hovel and I've had enough of it. Had enough of living like this.'

The heroine's sister had just revealed she was

expecting a baby. Ethel's face registered unqualified approval. Her lips at the end of the cigarette formed the words, 'Bless her.'

'I'm walking out of this house tonight and I'm not coming back, d'you hear me? I'll probably pick up with one of those girls who hang about the park gates and spend the night with her. Tomorrow I'll find somewhere else to stay, then go down to the Social Services and tell 'em I've left this address. Once that's done you won't catch me in this place any more.' The thought of the imminent change in his way of life pleased Arthur and he chortled. 'Yes, that's what I'll do. Then I'll find a smart young piece to set up with. One with long hair, hanging in a horse's tail right down her back.' He raised his voice. 'Someone who doesn't put those bleedin' hedgehogs in her hair.'

Ethel turned her head in what began as a gesture of reproof, but the programme won. After giving him a brief blank look, she returned her attention to the television screen.

'There won't be any television in the next place I'm in, either. We'll have a bit of interesting conversation now and again. Talk about things that are happening in the world. Politics and horse-racing. We might even go to see one of them symferny concert things, like they have in the park on a Sunday afternoon. I'll learn to live a full and worthwhile life.' As he was talking, Arthur was unconsciously scraping some of the previous day's breakfast from his waistcoat with a thumb nail. 'I should have done this years ago. I just don't know how I've

135

put up with all this for so long.'

Some of his initial enthusiasm had worn off, but when he looked at Ethel, it flooded back once more. 'You just bleedin' well stop here and rot, like you've been doing for all these years. I don't need you — and I don't want you. I'm off, right now.'

Lifting his jacket from the back of a chair, he pushed his right arm inside a sleeve, then swung the jacket around so it was in a position to take his left arm. This involved a considerable struggle as his arm kept going inside the lining, instead of into the sleeve. Eventually he won and fastened three buttons, forcing the two edges of the jacket to meet, albeit reluctantly, in three places.

'I'm going now, do you hear me?'

The only response came from Ethel's cigarette. A thumb-nail length of ash fell down between her knees to join the powdered remains of earlier cigarettes.

Turning away, Arthur stomped from the room and along the passageway. As the street door crashed shut, Ethel turned a disinterested glance in that direction.

Thirty seconds later there was the sound of a key in the lock of the front door and a somewhat subdued Arthur returned to the room. His silence had more effect upon Ethel than had his shouting. Waving a hand towards the cluttered table, she said, 'If it's yer false teeth yer after, they're where yer left 'em. On the saucer, next to yer teacup.'

Arthur picked up his forgotten teeth. Popping

them in his mouth, he manoeuvred them into position with his tongue.

'No, love, it's not me teeth, but thanks all the same.' He sniffed apologetically. 'It's just . . . I've run out of money. Lend me a couple of quid until I pick up the dole money tomorrow, will you? I know you've got it. I saw the postman come today.'

He was practically grovelling.

'You're a clever old stick really, love,' he said. 'I just don't know where we'd be if it wasn't for your writing. Doing the weekly 'Health and Beauty' column for that women's magazine.'

A Girl Like Fionna

The wild, rugged coastline of north-west Scotland is inhabited by communities who have wrested a living from the sea for countless generations. Fishing villages are to be found huddling at the base of towering cliffs, sheltering on the shores of a deep-water loch and clinging precariously to the side of a steep hill.

One of the latter is the village of Galbraith.

Its narrow streets zig-zag down to the sea, bringing to mind a fun-fair gaming machine, of the type which disgorges a ball that will run to and fro along descending metal chutes to finally drop into a prize-winning cup at the base of the machine.

But on one hot, thundery summer's day, it was not a ball that ran down the narrow streets of Galbraith.

It was a rumour. Bursting forth from the coastguard station at the top of the hill, it tumbled helter-skelter from house to house, gathering speed and substance, like a snowball. Enveloping the quay where the inshore boats lay, it sped on, to the long stone jetty where the deep-sea trawlers would tie up when they were not at sea. Here it burst, scattering its message among the men who worked on their boats.

'Jamie McPherson is lost. His boat is believed to have sunk in a violent summer storm, off Fair Isle.'

Fair Isle! The mere mention of the inappropriately named island sent a chill through the bones of the fishermen here. No more than a mere dot on the map, between the Shetland and Orkney Islands, it had claimed the lives of many good men from these communities.

The news stunned the whole village. Jamie was a huge red-haired man, beloved by the whole community. With his uncanny knack of finding the herring, he had brought pride and prosperity to Galbraith. Dissatisfied with fishing in a small way, Jamie had taken himself off to Aberdeen when he was eighteen years old. By the age of twenty-two he was a skipper and when he returned to Galbraith at the age of twenty-five, he was the owner of his own, brand-new trawler.

Men had been lost from the village before. Jamie's father among them. But all who had sailed with the young man proudly proclaimed he was the best fisherman the village had ever known. The loss of a boat was a tragedy that was felt by the whole community, but none had hit them harder than this, for Saturday was to have been Jamie's wedding day.

In the streets, the women quickly formed small, low-voiced groups, whispering their disbelief. There was a deeper sorrow in many of the homes too, for Jamie's crew was also from the village.

Inside one tiny cottage, on the first street up the hill behind the quay, a woman sat in a wooden rocking-chair, her work-worn hands alternately clutching and releasing the folds of a rough, tweed skirt. She was seated, but not at

142

rest. Moaning quietly, in anguish, she rocked steadily backwards and forwards. The young woman kneeling by her side tried to comfort her, fingers resting lightly on the older woman's arm.

'Hisht, Mother. He'll be back, I know he will. There have been other storms. Worse than this one. Just quiet yourself, Jamie will be back.'

The gentle voice, with its soft Scots accent was soothing enough, but the other woman seemed not to hear. Many years ago she had lost her man in just such a storm. Now it was her son. No words of his intended bride would bring back either of them. This she knew because she had lived through it all before.

Realising the futility of her attempts to comfort the widow, the young woman stood up, smoothing down the folds of her plaid skirt. 'Stay here, Mother. I'll away to the Bonnie Prince to see what the news is.'

There were no tears on Fionna Jamieson's face. No sign to show what she felt inside. She strode along the streets, ignoring the women who ceased their chatter to nod sympathetically as she passed. She held her head high as she walked. Jamie would be home for the wedding. He had told her so. He would not let her down, as her father had so tragically failed her mother. Twenty years ago preparations for another wedding had been far advanced when her own father had been lost. The laws of procreation would not be denied, even by such a tragedy. Fionna had been born, six months later, without a church service to bless her entry into the small community. She refused to accept that cruel fate

143

and the sea would rob her of the thin cloak of respectability twice in her short lifetime. Jamie would not allow it to happen.

As Fionna entered the crowded bar-room, the buzz of conversation ceased abruptly. Surprise, resentment even, registered on the faces of the men. Women — nice women — were never seen inside a bar in this part of the world. Fionna ignored their disapproval. Her direct gaze fell upon a large-boned, bearded man standing at the far end of the room, a huge pewter tankard clutched in his hand.

'Will you please tell me what the news is, Mr Cameron?'

She spoke in an even voice.

Roderick Cameron, acknowledged leader of the little community, cleared his throat noisily before answering.

'It's not good, lass.' His deep, bass voice boomed out in the smoke-hazed atmosphere. 'The radio station at Wick picked up part of a disjointed Mayday signal, and rockets were seen between Fair Isle and the Orkneys by a fishing-boat which was too fully laden to turn in such seas. A lifeboat was launched, but had to return with engine trouble. It's the worst weather they've had up there for many a year. Jamie's boat was believed to be the only one in the area at the time. He left the main fishing fleet yesterday, so as to be back early for the wedding . . . '

He stopped abruptly, afraid that mention of the wedding would cause Fionna to dissolve in a flood of tears, but her expression never changed.

144

'I've heard all that,' she said. 'I'm here to ask what you and the other men are going to do about it?'

The big man flushed. 'That's what we're meeting about now. This is men's business, Fionna.'

Fionna looked scornfully around the room before she spoke again. 'And how many drinks will it take before you decide to *do* something?'

Her words brought an angry murmur that grew louder from the men. The fishermen were resentful of this slip of a girl. She had not only invaded their male sanctuary, but was trying to tell them what they should be doing.

Roderick Cameron started to say something, but was interrupted by the sound of a mug being banged noisily on a wooden table in the corner of the room. All eyes turned towards the man who was causing the sound. A small, white-haired fisherman, his wrinkled, ruddy face spoke of a lifetime divided between his two loves. The sea — and good Highland whisky.

'The lass is right,' he said, placing his pipe down upon the table in front of him. 'We all know what needs to be done. We need to put to sea and find him. Let's have no more talk. Away to the boats and leave the blathering to the women.'

A growing murmur of approval greeted the short speech. Fionna looked at the old man gratefully.

But Roderick Cameron was calling for silence. 'That's easier said than done,' he shouted, above the din. 'You know well enough that the fleet is at sea. The only boats left are the cranky ones. We need to find out how many boats are fit to put out.'

Fionna gave him a withering look. 'You be doing that, Mr Cameron. In the meantime I'll away to the jetty and take a boat out myself — and don't think I *can't* do it. No doubt when I've found him you'll still be in here, arguing and drinking.'

Before a scarlet-faced Roderick Cameron could reply, a man shouted from the crowd, 'Good for you lass. You'll not need to take yourself to sea. My boat will be out there within the half-hour.'

Another fisherman stood up, quickly followed by more. Within a minute seven boats were pledged to take part in the search. The shouts of other men criss-crossed the room as they volunteered to go out as crewmen in the search for Jamie.

One by one the trawlers cast off their mooring ropes and headed out in the choppy waters of the loch. Some had not been to sea for weeks. Others rarely ventured beyond sight of the rocky coast, but they would be seaworthy in all but the most violent weather. Their slow-throbbing engines echoed back from the surrounding hills as, one after another, they headed for the open sea.

On the jetty, womenfolk, and the men who for one reason or another were unable to go to sea, stood and watched until the boats passed out of sight. The crowd was thickest around Jamie's mother and Fionna. Every few minutes one of the villagers would edge across to Mrs McPherson and, avoiding Fionna's eyes, offer a few words of consolation. On each occasion, Fionna would say confidently, 'There's no need to fret yourself. Jamie will be back. Are you forgetting we have a wedding on Saturday?'

The women would look at her pityingly, then turn away, shaking their heads. 'Poor lass,' they would say. 'Poor wee lass. It's hard for her, losing her man so close to their wedding day, but she'll learn to accept it — the same as her mother did.'

Fionna would not accept it. Not even on Friday, when all the trawlers limped back to Galbraith, battered and mauled by the aftermath of the storm in which Jamie had been lost.

The fishermen, weary and strained after their futile search, averted their eyes from the tall, straight figure who stood waiting, her clothes whipping around her in the wind which was beginning to pick up again, sending spray high over the jetty, even here in the sheltered loch.

Roderick Cameron's boat was the last to return. He trudged wearily along the jetty towards her, the memory of their last meeting forgotten. All resentment had been drained from him by the days and nights spent searching the open, empty sea.

Laying a large arm across her shoulders, he tried to draw her away, back to the village. 'Come along, lass. Everything that could be done, has been. Jamie would be proud of your tenacity, but it's no good. No boat could have lasted in the storm they've had out there. Had his boat been afloat, we'd have found it. Away

147

with you now to your bed. You look as though you could do with sleep as much as any of us.'

'I thank you, Mr Cameron,' she said, no flicker of emotion on her pale face. 'I'll bide here a while. Jamie will be back for our wedding. I know he will.'

She stayed there until far into the night, listening as the wind died away and calm returned to land and sea. When the sun came up over the hills the air was soft and warm. It was as though the elements were ashamed of the display of temper shown to Scotland during the past few days. Only now did Fionna return to the house and shut herself in her bedroom. She remained there, even when she heard the villagers leaving their homes and making their way to the little kirk on the hill. Instead of a wedding, there was to be a memorial service for Jamie and his crew.

In their sombre black clothes, the fisherfolk walked along the street, past her house. In the subdued voices she detected strong disapproval. She was Jamie's girl — yet she was one of only a handful in the village who would not be attending the memorial service. How could she tell them that, even now, she refused to believe he was dead?

Not until she heard their voices coming to her through the open door of the kirk, rising and falling to the simple tune of a hymn, did Fionna break.

She made no sound. There were no tears. Just a sudden, desperate feeling of hopelessness. Jamie *had* to be dead. Nothing else would have kept him from the wedding. With Jamie went all her hopes for the future. Her dreams of enjoying love and respectability at last. Without him there was nothing.

She ran out on the street, hair streaming behind her, until she reached the jetty. There was a boat moored here and she tumbled into it, sobbing noisily now. Grasping the oars, she rowed out in the loch, away from the village and its mourners. There was no plan in her mind. She only knew she was going to join Jamie. That was all.

Inside the kirk, the service had almost come to an end when the villagers heard the sound. It was one they had heard a thousand times. Part of the life of a fishing village — but never before had it produced such an effect upon them. The flat throb of the trawler's engine was not very loud at first. Only a few of those closest to the open door heard it. But gradually the sound came closer. Eventually, it reached the preacher who was holding forth on the virtues of the missing men. He faltered, said a few more words, then stopped altogether.

A small boy, more venturesome than the rest, broke from the pews at the back of the kirk and darted out through the open door. The congregation waited with bated breath until the excited shout came back to them. 'It's Jamie! He's here. He's here with another boat in tow.' The service broke up in chaos as the villagers rushed from the kirk, down the hill to the water's edge.

Closing on the jetty was Jamie's trawler. Its mast snapped off, the deck was a shambles of ruined fishing gear. Behind it, on the end of a wire cable, gunwales almost awash, was the wreck of another trawler, Scandinavian in appearance. From the bridge of the towing vessel, a familiar red-headed figure waved cheerfully to those on shore.

As the two boats came alongside, ropes came curving across the water and there were many willing hands to catch them and make them fast. Even before the boats had berthed, questions and answers were being shouted back and forth.

'Are all your crewmen safe?'

'Aye — but it was a terrible storm.'

'No, the Mayday message was not from us.'

When Jamie stepped ashore, the villagers crowded about him and his crew and he told them what had happened to them.

The Mayday picked up by the radio station had come from the Scandinavian trawler, as had a number of distress rockets. Jamie had taken his trawler to the rescue and somehow managed to take the other boat in tow. The two vessels had sheltered in the lee of an uninhabited Orkney island until the storm had cleared. During the rescue, his trawler had been dismasted and a huge wave poured gallons of water into the compartment housing the radio batteries, completely destroying radio communications.

In the midst of the happy chatter, someone asked where Fionna was. The ensuing uncomfortable silence was broken by Jamie himself.

'She's all right,' he said. 'Something must have told her I was coming in. I found her rowing to meet us, almost a mile up the loch. A little farther and she'd have been in open sea — and would have no doubt capsized. The last few days must have been a terrible strain for her. She's asleep in my cabin right now.'

He looked over the crowd to where the preacher stood, Bible clutched in his hand. 'I'm sorry I'm late for the wedding, Mr McAllister, but I hope it won't upset our plans too much. Shall we make it for six o'clock tonight? I said today would be my wedding day, and so it shall. I'm not a man to break a promise. Especially when it's made to a girl like Fionna.'

A Case of Spirits

I had always read news items which told of people becoming lost whilst hiking across the moors with a certain amount of irritation. So unnecessary, I thought. A few simple precautions and it need never have happened. At least, those were my views until it happened to me.

It was during a holiday I spent in Ireland — a most delightful country. I left my hotel in the small village of Killynorn after enjoying an early breakfast and set out across the rolling moors, my knapsack slung over my shoulder. All that morning I tramped, taking careful note of the landmarks I passed. A tall tree here; a peculiar shaped hill there. I even took careful bearings from the sun.

Shortly after noon I discovered a lovely little valley, with a brook, chuckling merrily over a gravel bed, running along the whole of its length. Here I had my lunch. It was so peaceful I remained there for almost two hours. I even had a little nap, but I woke with a sudden start to realise the sun was no longer sparkling on the crystal clear water. The little valley had lost its warm, bright appeal. It was now a sombre, grey place, that was somehow far less pleasant. Looking up I saw dark, menacing clouds scudding overhead.

Hastily replacing the remains of my meal inside my knapsack, I scrambled up the side of the valley and was alarmed to see a belt of rain sweeping towards me across the moors. Already, more than half the landmarks I had so meticulously plotted had disappeared from view. Hurriedly, I set out for one that was still visible. A solitary tree standing on a small rise, about half a mile distant. Long before I reached it the storm was upon me. The heavy drops of rain struck at my face, stinging my cheeks. I put on the light plastic raincoat I had brought with me, but I had no hat. Soon my hair was soaked and rivulets were running from it, down my neck and inside the collar of my shirt.

I never did find the landmark. After searching this way and that for an hour, I gave up the impossible task. The rain had not abated. I decided the only sensible thing to do was find some form of shelter and wait, hoping the storm would soon clear.

It seemed luck had deserted me with the sun. Three hours later I was still seeking a place of refuge. True, the rain was not falling with its earlier intensity. It had settled into a heavy drizzle. Nevertheless I was wandering aimlessly in a grey world, aware only of wet, spongy turf beneath my feet. I was thoroughly miserable too. So much so that the realisation I was hopelessly lost was no longer my major concern. I could think only of finding shelter from the weather.

Then I realised that the ground beneath my feet was no longer soft and springy, but crunched solidly as I walked. I was on some sort of track! It was evidently not well-used. The number of large clumps of grass I stumbled over along the way told me that. But a path in this part of the country, however old, had to lead somewhere. I followed it with all the eagerness of a beagle on the scent.

It was descending now and ahead of me I could see a dark shadow, through the drizzle. As I came closer it materialised into a small wood, with tall trees that met over the path. In themselves they formed a shelter of sorts, despite heavy drops of water that slid from their leaves. But my eyes were fixed upon what lay beyond them. It was a house!

In other circumstances it would probably not have appeared to be particularly welcoming. Dull, grey stone walls and a darker grey slate roof were in themselves sombre enough. Add to this shuttered windows and a generally neglected appearance and you have a house with a somewhat brooding air. However, there was light shining through a chink in one of the downstairs shutters. Someone was in occupation.

I squelched up the steps to the front door. It was a stout wooden affair set with studs and with stout iron hinges. Lifting the heavy iron ring which served as the door-knocker, I brought it down heavily. Once, twice, three times. The sound echoed within the house. I had to repeat the operation twice more before I heard movement inside the house. Then there was the grating sound of bolts being drawn and, to the accompaniment of a quartet of protesting hinges, the door slowly swung open.

I am not quite sure who I had expected to reside in this rather grim-looking house, but I was pleasantly surprised. Standing before me was a cheery-faced little old man. He broke into a gnome-like smile that made him appear years younger than he really was.

'Why,' he said, in a strong Irish brogue, ''Tis a stranger come visiting. Come in, will you. Come in. I'm sorry I was so long in opening the door. I thought it was 'them' playing me up again.' He made no attempt to explain who 'them' were, but hustled me into the room from which I had seen light shining through the shutter.

It was a small room, rather over-cluttered with the type of furniture that had been popular many decades before. It smelled cosily of wood smoke from the fire crackling merrily in the grate. There were paraffin fumes too, from a lamp smoking away in the corner of the room.

The little man fussed over my bedraggled appearance. 'Dear me. Dear me! You poor fellow. 'Tis soaking wet you are. Be getting them wet things off and I'll bring you a blanket. Here, pull this chair up to the fire. You'll be catching your death of cold if we're not careful.' With much effort he pulled a great stuffed armchair close to the fire then hurried from the room.

I heard his footsteps ascending the stairs. Then there was the muffled sound of voices, as though he was having an argument with someone. He returned a couple of minutes later, carrying a large, soft blanket in his arms.

Stripping off my sodden clothes, I wrapped myself in the blanket and settled myself before the fire, allowing the warmth to soak in to my shivering body. The old man carried my clothes

158

from the room, muttering something about getting them dried out. When he reappeared, he went to a large, dark-wood cabinet in the corner of the room. Taking out two large glasses, he filled them from a bottle that bore no label.

'Here,' he said, handing me a glass of light brown liquid. 'Get this inside you. It's good Irish whiskey — but don't be asking me any questions as to where it comes from.' The first mouthful of the fiery liquid made me cough and splutter. When it went down it left a warm glow to mark its passage.

'This is excellent whiskey,' I said. 'I don't think I've ever tasted better.'

'Of course you haven't,' the old man replied. 'That's because there *is* no better. We've been making it like that for years. If them swindlers up in the city could get the recipe for it they'd make themselves a fortune, so they would. Now then, what are you doing way out here, in the state you were? Would you be lost?'

I smiled ruefully. 'I'm afraid I am. I left Killynorn this morning to go for a walk on the moors. When the rain came I lost my way.'

'I should say you did!' he said. 'You can thank your lucky stars you found this house. There isn't another for miles around. If you had wandered another mile to the east you would have been in the bog. There's not many men have found their way out of there, I can tell you.'

He shook his head sadly. 'On a fine night you can still hear the cries of the Duke's men who were lost there almost three hundred years ago. Not a man of them got away.'

Looking at me sharply, he added, 'D'you know you're the first Englishman to set foot in this house since that self-same Duke came here and put everyone to the sword?' The intensity of his stare startled me. It must have shown on my face because he laughed. 'Oh, you needn't be worrying yourself. At least, not as far as I'm concerned. Sean O'Neil never hurt a soul. But I think I'd better be keeping an eye on you while you're here.'

Something in his manner disturbed me. I was about to speak when I saw he seemed to have forgotten my presence. He was in what might almost have been a trance.

He remained in this condition for fully five minutes and I sat watching him, feeling extremely ill at ease. Then, as suddenly as he had drifted into this suspended state, he returned. A quick shake of his head and the bright button eyes were fixed on me once more.

'Do you believe in spirits?' he asked, suddenly.

Feeling there was a great deal behind this enquiry, I thought carefully before replying.

'Well,' I said, hesitantly, 'it's not a subject I have had a great deal of experience with. I believe we all have a great deal to learn about such things — but I certainly don't *disbelieve* in them.'

To my intense relief, he seemed satisfied with my reply. 'Good!' he nodded. 'That's good. There's nothing upsets them quite so much as not being believed in.'

Feeling extremely nervous, I looked quickly around the room. 'You mean . . . there are spirits here? In this house?'

'Why, bless you, yes,' the little man said, matter-of-factly. 'I told you when I was so long coming to open the door that I thought it was them. Always playing tricks like that they are. Getting me to open a door for them when they can walk through it with no trouble at all. That's one of young Michael's favourite tricks, that is.'

'Young Michael?' I queried, feebly.

'That's right,' said my host, cheerfully. 'I always call him *young* Michael so as not to confuse him with his father, you understand. They were both killed by the Duke's men. Good as gold they are really, y'know — unless some of them soldiers from the bog wander across here. Then 'tis like Saturday night at the village hall.'

He chuckled so much he broke into a fit of coughing. Rising to his feet, he hurried across the room and I watched his progress with a certain amount of apprehension.

I breathed a sigh of relief when he opened the cupboard in the corner and poured out two more large whiskeys. Taking a glass from his hand, I carried it to my mouth and swallowed considerably more than I had intended. 'You must remember this is not that cheap city stuff,' he said as he thumped my back to relieve my choking. 'Treat it like a lady. With respect.'

Wiping my eyes on a corner of the blanket, I said, hopefully, 'These, er . . . 'spirits' you were talking about. They are quite harmless?'

'Oh yes,' said the old man, 'quite harmless . . . at least,' he added, thoughtfully, 'most of them are.'

161

'*Most* of them?' I repeated, weakly.

'Yes — though there's some I wouldn't like to cross. Old Katie, for one.'

'Old Katie?' I queried.

'Nasty nature, she has. Murdered three husbands, y'know. She was hung on one of those big trees out front. They caught her when she tried to kill her fourth. Tied a piece of rope across the top of the stairs at night, she did. She's never been able to understand why it failed that last time. She keeps coming back to try it out again. You need to be very careful on the stairs at night. Very careful indeed.'

My mouth must have hung open for quite a long time. When the old man looked up, he said, 'Come on then, me boy, you're hardly touching the whiskey. It isn't often I have company, y'know. Not the company of a man like yourself, that is. I talk to them, of course, but you can't get much sense out of them. Too wrapped up in their own problems, I suppose.'

He looked all about him with a sly look on his puckish round face and lowered his voice to a conspiratorial whisper.

'The one you *really* want to look out for is Sir Dermot.' He looked at me anxiously. 'None of your ancestors were executioners, were they?'

I hurriedly thought of all the ancestors I could recall, fervently wishing I had delved deeper into my genealogical tree.

'None that I can recall,' I replied.

He nodded, but I felt his reply lacked real conviction. 'Oh well, you'll probably be all right. You see, Sir Dermot had his head taken off on the block for leading some uprising against the English. He's very put out about it. Very put out. He walks around the bedrooms, lifting up the bedclothes and peering at anyone who might be asleep there, hoping to find the executioner.'

The old man shook his head. 'Very disconcerting, it is. It wouldn't be so bad if he made the effort and held his head where it should be, on his shoulders, you understand? It beats me why he goes to so much trouble. Even if he found the man, I doubt if there's very much could be done to repair the damage now.'

Knocking back the last of his whiskey, my host said, 'I've told him so many a time. 'Sir Dermot,' I've said, 'let bygones be bygones. The poor man was only doing his job. I doubt if he enjoyed it any more than you did,' I've said. But he won't listen. Come to that, I don't even know if he can hear me. Not with his head held the way he has it sometimes, I don't.'

I was sweating a little now, even though the fire had almost burned itself out.

The old man stood up. 'Well, I've no doubt you'll be wanting to take yourself to bed.'

Despite my experiences earlier in the day I was not at all certain I did want to go to bed. Not in this house, anyway. Unfortunately, there seemed to be very little I could do about it.

Toddling over to the cupboard once more, the old man filled the two glasses for a third time.

'Just a little nightcap,' he explained. 'Be drinking that and I'll fetch your clothes. I put them in the chimney cupboard. They should be dry by now.'

While he was away I glanced anxiously around the room, my nerves very much on edge. When one of the charred logs in the grate collapsed, I jumped up, spilling my whiskey over the blanket.

Thankfully, when the old man returned with my clothes, they were completely dry and quite warm. He brushed my thanks aside as I put them on. "'Tis nothing. If we can't help one another it's a very sad world. I've just looked outside. The rain has cleared and the moon is trying to come through. It will be quite fine by morning. You'll just need to follow the track all the way and you'll be in Galrea in no time. You can catch a bus from there to Killynorn. But I'll be up with you, so you don't have to worry. Are you ready for bed now?'

I said I was. Clutching my outdoor clothes in one hand and carrying the blanket, I followed the old man as he went ahead of me carrying the smoking paraffin lamp. He picked his way carefully up the stairs, pausing at the top to bend down and examine the stair more closely. His examination completed, he turned a cheerful face to me. 'It's all right,' he said, 'Katie hasn't been around tonight. There's no rope there.'

I was greatly relieved by his statement. Nevertheless, I felt about with my foot before I finally placed it upon the fatal step.

While I was doing this the old man had gone ahead along a dark passageway and opened a door at the end of it. With a sudden shout he disappeared inside the room. The door slammed behind him and I was left alone in the darkness of the passage. To make matters worse, I dropped some of my clothes on the floor.

My host was making a lot of noise in the room. 'No you don't!' I heard. 'I've told you before, I'll put up with none of your tricks. I'll have you this time, so I will.' His shouting was accompanied by a great deal of banging and crashing. All this time I stood in the passageway, too scared even to bend down and find my missing clothes.

Eventually, the noises ceased and the door to the room opened. 'Did you see him?' the old man asked, breathlessly. 'Did he come out this way?'

'No,' I said, a tremor in my voice. 'Wh-who w-was it?'

'It was Michael,' he replied. 'He must have gone through the other wall. Mind, he was only up to a little mischief. Making up an apple-pie bed for me. The trouble is, you let him get away with something like that and it'll be far worse the next time. Never mind, don't let it be bothering you. He's gone now. But it's a good thing you'll be sleeping in the same room as myself. You can never tell what they'll be getting up to next.'

He stopped, holding one finger in the air as inspiration came to him. 'I've just had a fine idea. Can you speak with an Irish accent?'

I looked doubtful.

'Try,' said the old man, looking quite excited. 'Let me hear you say something.'

My mind in turmoil, I desperately sought for something to say. 'Er . . . it's a braw, bricht, moonlicht nicht, the nicht,' I said, in despair.

He looked disappointed. 'No, I don't think

165

we'd fool any of them with that. Never mind, I'm sure you'll be all right. Come in the bedroom.'

Retrieving my clothing from the floor, I followed him in to the room.

Even in my present state of mind I was forced to admit there was nothing frightening about it. The room contained two single beds, one rather rumpled — hardly surprising, I thought, in view of the recent disturbance. However, apart from a considerable amount of junk strewn around — a couple of tennis racquets, a pair of boxing gloves, an ancient gramophone and a huge pile of records — it seemed quite ordinary.

Once we were in the room the old man ignored me. Going to the gramophone, he wound the handle vigorously. Then, sorting through the records, he selected one and placed it upon the turntable.

It was a very old record. The sound that emerged from the ear-trumpet-like speaker was so distorted it was impossible to identify the name, or even the sex of the singer. Yet, while it grated out sound, the old man sat on one of the beds and closed his eyes in ecstasy. He remained in this state until the record had stopped playing. Jumping up, he re-wound the machine and repeated the performance. When it ended for a second time, he again wound the gramophone, but this time he turned to me before he started it once more.

'Did you like that?' he asked.

I gave a mute nod of my head.

He nodded his head in approval. 'I'm glad. Then you won't mind if I play it again?'

166

Lowering his voice, he winked. 'It's not for me, you understand, but for *them*. Lulls them to sleep. Sometimes I play it three or four times and I don't hear a word from them all the night long.'

'Then by all means play it again,' I said fervently. 'Play it as many times as you like.'

'I think once more should do,' he said. 'But don't let me be keeping you up. Get yourself into bed. You've had a tiring day. Just a minute though, where's me manners?'

So saying, he dived beneath his bed and reappeared holding a bottle of whiskey, of the same type as that we had been drinking downstairs. Placing it on the floor behind him, he burrowed beneath the bed once more. After pulling out a variety of shoes, books and empty bottles, he produced two chipped cups.

'Knew they were there somewhere,' he explained, dusting them off with an old towel which had also been hiding beneath the bed.

'I have to keep it there, otherwise they find them. Especially Black Patrick. A terrible one for the bottle he is. Terrible! But I'd better not be telling you of him. Don't want you having nightmares, do we?'

I was certain I would not sleep a wink anyway, but I was grateful for his silence on the subject of Black Patrick. I did not think I could take in very much more.

The anonymous record was played over twice more, then the old man climbed into bed without taking any of his clothes off. Reaching over to the lamp, he was about to extinguish it

— a moment I had been secretly dreading — when he stopped. 'Would you like me to leave it on low?' he asked. 'In case you need to get up during the night?'

I tried not to sound too relieved when I agreed with his suggestion.

'Right you are. A very good night to you. Don't take too much notice of any noises you might hear. I don't think they'll be after hurting you. I'll be mightily surprised if they do.'

With this cheerful remark, he turned over and went to sleep.

I knew I would not be able to sleep myself, but I pulled the blanket up over my head and tried to think of all the pleasant things of life. Cities; comforting traffic noises; people on trains; crowded shops. Things like that. Occasionally I thought I heard a strange noise. Twice I fearfully raised my head from beneath the blanket, but saw nothing. After that I kept my head down and tried not to listen for sounds within the house.

I must have been half dozing when I suddenly heard a noise unlike all the others. It was much closer too. My nerves were drawn as taut as a yew bow as I listened. Yes, there was no doubt about it. I could hear footsteps. They seemed to slither along the ground somewhere very near at hand. There was a brief silence, then a swishing sound. It was followed by an unearthly, gurgling scream. With my hair standing on end, I heard the footsteps coming closer — and still closer.

Suddenly, my nerve snapped. I could stand it no longer. I flung off the bedclothes in a moment of sheer panic — and there stood the little old man.

'I'm sorry,' he said. 'Did I wake you? It's that old cistern, it makes a terrible noise. Old plumbing, you know.'

He climbed in his bed and pulled the bedclothes up around him and I sank back trembling. I would never be the same man again. I knew I wouldn't.

A few minutes later I was listening to the old man snoring. He must have had nerves of steel. How could he possibly sleep? The slightest noise set me off trembling. Then, somehow, the impossible happened. I dozed off. It must have been the drink taking effect. I don't think I would have believed it had I not been suddenly woken — by a blood-curdling scream. It was a moment or two before I realised the sound had come from my own throat. It felt as though I was being battered by all the demons in hell.

Sitting bolt upright, I saw the little old man again. He was dancing up and down with two tennis racquets in his hand, banging me into wakefulness. Thrusting one of the tennis racquets into my hand, he shouted, 'Quick, get up. There's a bat flying around in the room. Stand on your bed and I'll stand on mine. We'll get him. Hurry, before he gets away.'

I looked down at my racquet. There were no strings in it.

*   *   *

Dawn was breaking as I reached the village. Trudging along the quiet main street, I saw a farm labourer on his way to work. He stopped to talk to a policeman who was leaning lazily against his bicycle.

The policeman straightened up as I approached and both men looked at me with more than a passing curiosity.

'Excuse me, Officer,' I said wearily. 'I've been lost on the moors since yesterday morning. Could you tell me where I catch the bus to Killynorn?'

The policeman beamed at me. 'You'll be the Englishman — Mr Trelawney. You've been reported missing. We were going to go out looking for you this morning.'

Peering at me more closely, he added, 'If you'll pardon me for saying so, Sir, you're surprisingly dry, in view of the weather we've had out there on the moors.'

'Yes,' I said. 'I found a house and the gentleman there put me up for the night. But I decided to make an early start.'

The policeman and the farm labourer looked at each other in a puzzled manner.

'Someone put you up, you say?' said the policeman. 'Do you happen to know the name of the gentleman you stayed with?'

'Why yes, I do,' I replied. 'It was a Mr O'Neil. Sean O'Neil, I think he said.'

The policeman's face broke into a broad grin, as did that of the farmhand. 'Did you hear that?' he said, shaking his head in apparent reluctant admiration. 'The little fellow's gone and done it

170

again. I don't know how he manages it, I'm sure I don't.'

He carried on chuckling, shaking his head in amused disbelief until he caught my puzzled look.

'Oh, I'm sorry, Sir, you wouldn't be knowing, of course. You see, that house should be standing empty. Oh, it belongs to Sean O'Neil, all right, but he was committed to an asylum years ago. He's quite harmless, mind — but as mad as a hatter. Every so often he escapes, but we always know where to find him. He'll be back in his old house with his friends — the ghosts.'

The policeman chuckled again. 'Did he tell you about the ghosts, Sir?'

I took a deep breath, recalling the events of the night. 'No, Officer,' I said. 'No, I don't think he did.'

Chinese in Three Easy (?) Lessons

Have you ever tried to learn a language? I don't mean schoolboy French or Latin, but a real, living language — in the country where they speak it? If you decide to try your hand then perhaps I can offer you a hint or two.

When I first went into the family business I didn't have a care in the world. I certainly suffered no language difficulties. Our company manufactures cosmetics. In addition to the factory staff, it employs almost two hundred girl demonstrators in various towns and cities throughout the country. My job was to control these demonstrators, check on their work, recommend them for pay rises and so on. You don't need a vivid imagination to realise what a wonderful way of life it was.

Unfortunately, it came to a rather abrupt end. There was one particular girl who thought she was . . . well, no need to go into sordid detail. Suffice it to say I was transferred in a hurry. Sent to Hong Kong to expand the family business.

Once there, I decided that in order to make a success of things I would need to learn Chinese. The difficulty was knowing where to make a start.

My first attempt to master the language was brief, but illuminating.

I met up with Nui Tsai in one of those dance-halls where for the price of a ticket you can claim a girl's undivided attention for the duration of a dance. I bought a fistful of tickets, handed them all to Nui Tsai and guided her to a quiet corner table. Only then did I discover she did not speak English. Not that it really mattered. She had the sort of figure you speak about, not to.

She called the waiter and ordered drinks for us. I paid, of course. Without finding the lack of a common language embarrassing, we got through a few drinks and a few dances. Then she called the waiter to the table once more. This time she rattled away to him in Chinese — and it wasn't the usual 'I want a drink' talk.

'What was that all about?' I asked the waiter when Nui Tsai ceased talking.

'She say she have pain in head,' said the waiter in a high-pitched voice. 'Would like for you to take her out from here.'

'Fine!' I rose to my feet. 'Ask her what she's waiting for. Let's go.'

'Is not so easy,' the waiter replied, shaking his head. 'First you must pay money to take her out. You see, owner of dance-hall lose money if all girls go out with their men.'

'Fair enough,' I said, taking out my wallet. 'How much . . . ?'

Before the waiter had time to reply, Nui Tsai took the wallet from my hand, extracted about fifty dollars and handed them to the waiter, talking to him very quickly and waving him off. Clutching the money, the waiter bowed himself away. Nui Tsai took my hand and led me outside. I thought we would be going straight to

176

Nui Tsai's place, but she had other ideas.

Hailing a passing taxi, we climbed in and she gave him directions — in Chinese, of course. The taxi headed for a section of town that I had been warned about. However, instead of turning up one of the narrow, climbing streets to the residential quarter, the driver went the other way. Towards the waterfront. When we eventually stopped we were close to a small jetty. Moored alongside were dozens of sampans — small Chinese boats.

While I was paying off the taxi, Nui Tsai wandered off along the jetty. I caught up with her just in time to get out my wallet once more and part with more dollars. This time it was to a woman who owned a sampan. With the aid of a single oar, secured to the stern, she would provide the power to take us for a trip out in the harbour. Once on the water I discovered a whole new world I had never known about before. The world of the boat people.

Gently propelled around the fringes of the colourful harbour, we were entertained by a floating orchestra, supplied with drinks from a floating bar and bought food from a sampan that swayed and dipped in the wake of a passing ship, yet still managed to produce deliciously cooked seafood. Then, by the strangest of coincidences we met up with a sampan in which were a number of Nui Tsai's friends.

Two of them, a Chinese boy and his giggling girlfriend, came aboard our sampan. They brought with them a box containing a large number of oblong ivory pieces upon which were engraved Chinese characters and other complicated designs. This, I would later discover, was a game called mah-jong. A great favourite with Chinese of all ages.

When the Chinese boy came aboard and he greeted me with a very correct 'Good evening', I thought I was going to have someone to talk to. Unfortunately, it seemed his English was limited to commenting on the goodness of morning, afternoon and evening. Nevertheless, the lack of communication did not prevent us from having a most enjoyable few hours playing this most Chinese of games.

Mah-jong is a gambling game, so we bought a few boxes of matches from a passing sampan, shared the matches out evenly and played happily using them as our stakes. I must have lost countless boxes of them by the time we returned to the jetty. It was then that an acrimonious argument began.

I could not translate the finer points of their diatribe, but it did not require an interpreter to inform me we had not been playing just for the fun of it. I was given to understand that each match represented one dollar. It would seem I owed them a quite incredible sum of money.

Fortunately, at the height of the argument a taxi came coasting by. Hailing it, I leaped inside and told the driver to get the hell out of there. As he screeched away in a haze of burning rubber, I heard Nui Tsai shrieking at me. The words she used were not ones I could ever repeat in polite company, but I had learned Chinese lesson number one.

Realising that such an unpleasant situation would have never arisen had I possessed a working knowledge of the language, I decided to learn Chinese by more orthodox means. Looking through the newspapers, I saw an advertisement from a prospective university student. It offered Chinese lessons in return for an opportunity to practice speaking English. I went to the address that was given and met the advertiser. Mai Lai was a most attractive eighteen-year-old girl.

We suited each other very well. So began an association that was both delightful and fruitful. Mai Lai taught me the Chinese language, while I like to feel I taught her a few things in return.

The lessons came to an abrupt end due to a most unfortunate misunderstanding. Mai Lai thought her mother and father had gone out to an official function which was not due to end until the early hours of the following morning. In fact, it had been cancelled. When the door opened and her father walked in to a room not usually associated with study, we were found in what I believe is referred to in Victorian novels as 'a compromising situation'.

Beyond ordering me out of the house, her father had very little to say at the time. However, the following day he called me to his office and made up for his vocal shortcomings of the previous evening. He began by asking details of my earnings and prospects. Then he enquired about my family background and ended by requesting I make public the details of the proposed wedding between his daughter and myself as soon as we had agreed upon a date. Feeling that a holiday was overdue, I departed on a tour of Japan. It lasted for two months and I did not announce my return to Hong Kong.

I believe Mai Lai was very upset, but I knew I was doing the right thing. It isn't right that marriage should take away the opportunity for a girl to receive a university education.

My third Chinese lesson was the hardest of them all.

I met Jenny when I was returning from a business trip to Manila, in the Philippines. A hostess on the aircraft, she was most impressed with my command of the Chinese language.

We chatted as often as was possible on the journey. By the time we landed at Hong Kong airport I had her address and telephone number and had arranged to ring her that very evening. Never one to disappoint a young lady, I duly telephoned her and we met for a night on the town.

It was one of the most enjoyable few hours I had experienced during my long stay in the Far East. After an expensive meal in a plush restaurant, we went from night club to night club. Jenny would occasionally correct the way I pronounced some of the Chinese words, so I did not feel at all bad about marking the whole evening down to 'expenses'.

After that first evening, we saw each other quite regularly.

I never did learn much about her family, or her past, but it would have made very little difference. Her future was what really interested me — and I meant to have a say in it. In truth, I had fallen in love for the very first time. Really in love. Wedding bells, preachers, little gold bands and all that sort of thing.

That's why the manner in which it all ended hit me so hard.

I was in the habit of meeting her at the airport whenever she came in on a flight. Waiting for her to do whatever is required of an air hostess when she completes a flight, I would then take her home.

On that last occasion I was in the bar when I heard the arrival of her aircraft announced. Finishing my drink, I left the airport bar and took up a position at the arrivals route barrier. The passengers came through first, then the crew. A very tired-looking Jenny was among them, carrying a small suitcase. I gave her a hug and made to kiss her, as I usually did, but she turned her face away and looked anxiously around the concourse.

'What's the matter?' I asked. 'Is everything all right? You look tired.'

'Everything is all right,' she said.

Another quick look around her, then she thrust the suitcase into my hands.

'Be a darling and take this for me. Don't wait here. Go out to the car. I will be with you in a few minutes.'

Before I could ask any more questions, she had gone, walking towards the lift that would take her to the operational section of the airport building. Puzzled by her slightly offhand behaviour, I could think of nothing else to do but follow her instructions and wait for her in the car. Carrying the suitcase, I walked to the exit doors. As I swung them open and left the building, four large men fell in alongside and behind me. One of them took a firm grip on the suitcase.

'Here! What's the idea . . . ?' I began.

One of the men flashed a police warrant card in front of my eyes. 'Let's have no fuss, Sir. If you will accompany us to the police station I am sure we will be able to get things sorted out very quickly.'

Ignoring my protests that I was waiting for Jenny, they bundled me inside a waiting car and drove to a police station. Here, in my presence, they began to unpack the suitcase. Instead of the usual frilly bits and pieces that a woman takes with her when spending a night away from home, there was a selection of my clothes. Jenny must have taken them from my room.

Then they pulled out a number of small packages, wrapped in plastic.

The largest of the policemen opened one of the packages and took out a pack containing a coarse white powder. Dipping a finger inside, he gingerly tasted the few specks clinging to it and pulled a wry face.

'What is it?' I asked, foolishly.

'Oh dear,' said the large policeman, 'I was hoping you could tell us all about it — and here you are saying you don't even know it's heroin.' With this observation he gave me a back-handed swipe that knocked me across the room. I trod on the toe of one of his companions and was promptly knocked back to the first policeman. By the time they had finished with me I felt decidedly groggy. In spite of my treatment I was unable to tell them anything about the heroin, for the very simple reason that I knew nothing.

I was no more helpful in court. When Jenny stepped up to the witness box, dressed as though she was on afternoon leave from a convent school, I realised that nothing I said would make any difference. They would believe her, not me.

She told the court she was sorry. She had never seen the packets before. At this stage the court proceedings were halted for a while while Jenny was comforted and her tears mopped up. When she recovered sufficiently to give evidence once more, she said she had been so much in love with me she had never dreamed of questioning it when I asked her to collect a suitcase from the hotel where I claimed to have left it, when I was last in Manila. Had she had the slightest suspicion of what was in the suitcase, she would have had nothing at all to do with it — or me.

There was a lot more evidence in the same vein. When she concluded, the judge said he hoped it had not been too much of an ordeal for her.

Oh yes, they believed her all right.

Taking into account the fact that I was a first offender, I believe I was unlucky to receive an eight-year sentence.

I had someone from the Prison Welfare section visit me in my cell yesterday. He thought I might like to start a course of studies while I was in prison. Offered to make arrangements for me to learn another language.

A Piper's Lament

I have just switched off the television set for the third time today and am rapidly losing my patience. If I had a telephone I would ring the television company and tell them exactly what I think of them.

They will insist on showing those confounded Highland Games. I will be glad when they are over. It seems that every time I switch on the set the Games are on and there *he* is. All six feet four of him, marching around in front of his pipe-band, chest thrown out and, of course, wearing his medal.

You must have seen him yourself. You might even know how Pipe Major Hector MacTavish came to win *that* medal, but the whole episode holds very painful memories for me.

I had known Hector before the war started. I was in the school pipe-band and he used to come to give us instruction. At that time he led the Kilcannock Municipal Pipe-Band. He could be seen strutting in front of them every Saturday afternoon, down at the football stadium. In fact, no Kilcannock social event was considered complete without Hector and his pipers. He thought quite a lot of himself, even in those days.

Actually, I might well have joined the band myself had it not been for the war. As it was, I volunteered for one of the Highland regiments, hoping to see a bit of action. Unfortunately, they discovered I was a piper and transferred me to the regimental pipe-band. I tried to tell them I had joined the army to be a soldier and not a bandsman, but you probably know the military mind. Volunteer for the Parachute Regiment and you'll most likely find yourself working in some underground bunker. I suppose to some people it would have seemed a grand way to fight a war. To me it was frustrating. The only time I went overseas was to a ceremonial parade in Belfast.

Until 1944, that is. Then, out of the blue, a draft arrived for the whole band. We were going to the Far East! It was at this time that our regular pipe major had the bad luck to break a leg playing football. And who do you think was sent to us as a replacement? Yes, that's right. Hector MacTavish. He had managed to keep out of the army until then. Some sort of reserved occupation, I believe. He was with us for some time before it was brought home to him that we were not the Kilcannock Municipal Pipe-Band.

He insisted upon carrying out intricate marching manoeuvres. And made himself very unpopular as a result.

'Before you know where we are,' my mate grumbled to me, one day, 'he'll be having us do the 'Gay Gordons' while we play.'

Such antics came to an abrupt end when the colonel, a regular soldier, caught him at it.

'MacTavish,' he said, scathingly, 'that fancy marching may be just the thing for a girls' band, or even on a dance floor — but this is the army. You will see to it that your pipers march in the

188

same manner as the regiment to which they belong.'

We had very little trouble with him after that.

It was early May when we boarded the troopship at Glasgow. Parading on the upper deck, we played the ship all the way down the Clyde. None of us knew for certain where we were going and there was much speculation as the ship zig-zagged its way across the oceans of the world.

We put Cape Town and Colombo behind us and then one morning awoke to find we had berthed in Sydney. Here we disembarked. For a few months it seemed we might as well have stayed in the United Kingdom. All we did was give innumerable performances for the benefit of the local population. The way things were going, I was quite certain the war would be over before we got to see any action. Then we were sent north, to that long chain of tiny islands that form part of what is now Indonesia. Here we played for battle-weary troops, to whom any form of entertainment was welcome. It was not exactly front-line stuff, but it was getting closer to it.

One day, an American general came along and asked if we would go to a small island some miles away and play for some of his troops.

'It's quite close to the battle area,' he said, a fat cigar rolling from one corner of his mouth to the other. 'But I know that won't worry you guys — and my soldiers would sure appreciate it.'

Naturally, the request was granted and arrangements made on the spot.

The Americans laid on a landing craft for us and we embarked all decked out in ceremonial dress. Fur busbies, the lot.

It was not the most comfortable of trips. The craft had a flat, steel bottom and flat, metal sides. The sun blazed down upon us and it felt as though we were sitting in a topless oven. The sea was quite choppy too and I have never been a good sailor.

We were not made any happier when we heard the soldier in charge of the boat, a stocky little sergeant, arguing with his second-in-command.

'Hell, Hank,' he said, spitting over the side. 'I thought you knew where this God-forsaken island was. You know damn well they all look the same to me.'

We seemed to have been bouncing about on the sea for hours. I was looking around for a convenient place in which to be sick, when the stocky sergeant called down to us.

'Hey, you guys! I think the island we are just coming to is the one, but I'm not absolutely certain. Do you want me and my buddy to go ashore first and make certain?'

Hector's face was a delicate shade of green. Like the rest of us, he had by now spent more than enough time aboard this uncomfortable means of transport. Standing up, he looked in the direction indicated by the American.

'You needn't bother,' he said. 'It's only a very wee island. We can't get lost there. Just run the boat up on the sand and we'll play our way ashore. I can't see anyone there to meet us, but they'll soon hear the pipes.'

We replaced our busbies, which had been removed on account of the heat, straightened ourselves up and the landing craft made its run in. There was a sudden surge of power as the craft reversed engines. A slight, grating bump beneath us. Then, with a noisy clatter, the ramp that formed the bow of the landing craft dropped down on the sand of the beach. Hastily forming up, we warmed up the pipes and, with Hector in the lead, we marched off the boat to the tune of 'Scotland The Brave'.

It was like walking straight into one of those travel posters you used to see stuck on the walls of cold, drab railway stations. A long stretch of golden sands, waving coconut palms and the sea breaking in soft white plumes before running gently up the beach. Ahead of us was a wide path, running back through the palms. Hector led us along it, the pipes sounding very loud as we marched between thick undergrowth on either side.

About two hundred yards farther along, the path widened out into a large clearing. Here were dozens of small huts, laid out with military precision. I was very surprised nobody came out to meet us, but I thought we had probably arrived in the middle of the troops' afternoon siesta. I think Hector was surprised too, but he kept us marching around the camp. No doubt his intention was to awaken the occupants.

It was not until we were circling the camp for the second time that any soldiers appeared. They did not come out of the huts, but from the jungle at the edge of the clearing. Lots and lots of little yellow men wearing sand-coloured uniforms, all with their hands held high in the air!

There was a wail of protests from the bagpipes as we stopped blowing and I thought I saw the Japanese officer in charge of the surrendering troops wince. He marched straight up to Hector, his five feet nothing dwarfed by the pipe major's huge bulk, and bowed ceremoniously.

'Please accept this sword of surrender,' he said, in fair English. 'My humble apologies that sword is not given by the Commanding Officer of this island. Unfortunately, when he saw you land with terrifying weapons that make noise like thousand cats, he found convenient tree behind which to commit himself to ancestors. Please, accept this sword. I go to join my men by the big hut. We sit there to await your pleasure.'

For the first time, Hector realised we had landed on an island that was still held by the enemy. I swear he would have fainted away with fright had not Andy McDonald and myself moved forward to support him. Andy led him away to sit in the shade of a nearby palm tree and I took the sword from the hands of the Japanese officer.

I thought he looked at the departing Hector with a peculiar expression on his face, so I said, 'Our commander is a very disappointed man. He thought we were going to have a marvellous battle, but you have surrendered without a fight. It is very sad.'

The Japanese officer accepted my explanation and gave a disconsolate shrug of his shoulders.

'We too were looking forward to a glorious fight — but against those weapons you have, the blood turns to water. Needing such huge men as yourself to carry them, they must indeed be terrible in battle. And the noise they make . . . Tell me, please, will the slight deafness I feel wear off soon? Or will it get worse?'

I reassured him and he trotted away to join his men who were seated quietly on the ground, averting their eyes from the 'terrible weapons' we were carrying.

One of the pipers was sent back to the landing craft to get off a signal explaining what had happened and Hector had fully recovered by the time an American landing party arrived a couple of hours later. In fact, I overheard him telling one of the American officers that he had seen the Jap soldiers as soon as we had landed but decided to carry on in the hope they could be drawn out into hand-to-hand combat.

As you can imagine, the newspapers around the world made a big thing of the incident. Particularly in America, where they carried such headlines as, 'Unarmed Scots Pipers Capture Pacific Island' and 'Scots Hero Captures Jap-held Island With Unarmed Pipe Band'.

Well, with headlines like that they had to give Hector a medal, didn't they?

Unfortunately, I was not around to tell them the real story. After spending a few days on board an American hospital ship, I was sent home. It was a most unfortunate accident and occurred in the landing craft on our way from the island. I had retained the Japanese officer's sword and, in a forgetful moment, had stood it point upwards against one of the seats.

A few minutes later, I sat down.

And they never even gave me a 'Mentioned in Despatches'.

From Rock and Tempest

The storm had been raging for more than twenty-four hours, pounding the boat unmercifully with bone-jarring ferocity. Standing, straddle-legged inside the wheel-house, Malcolm McFee, skipper of the fishing trawler *Bluebell*, felt weariness seeping to the very bones of his body.

They were now well into the second night of the tempest and the wind howled around the vessel with undiminished ferocity. It blew from the north-east and showed no sign of easing off. Indeed, the barometer had dropped another fraction during the last hour.

As the trawler pitched and tossed without respite, an occasional vivid flash of lightning illuminated the huge, mobile walls of green water. They towered high above the vessel, throwing frothy cream plumes of spume far into the darkness.

'I've not seen a sea like this for many years.'

Angus Fowler, a bearded and grizzled old fisherman spoke past the unlighted pipe gripped tightly between his teeth as he battled with the trawler's wheel, which the sea threatened to wrench from his grasp at any moment.

'Neither have I, Angus,' replied Malcolm. 'We would have to run into it on *Bluebell's* last trip. She's a bit too old to take on weather like this.'

'Aye,' growled Angus. 'It's a fine farewell to

197

the sea for you too. Do you think you'll be able to settle down to working in the head office after spending your life at sea, fishing?'

'I think so,' said Malcolm. He managed a tired grin. 'After all, I'll be a married man after Saturday. It will be nice to be going home to someone special every evening.'

'You're right there,' agreed Angus with an enthusiasm that belied his status as a confirmed bachelor. 'Young Janie Grant is a fine young lass. Doesn't she hail from somewhere along this part of the coast?'

'That's right,' said Malcolm. 'From Ardness. Her father's boat was lost with all hands some years ago, when she was a wee girl. Wrecked on the rocks just outside Ardness harbour. I suppose that's why she's so keen for me to give up the sea. I have no doubt there will be times when I shall miss this life, but I have ambitions, Angus. I'll gain nothing by remaining a fisherman all my life . . . '

Their conversation was cut short by the crash of the wheel-house door. Opening inwards, it slammed heavily against the bulkhead. Jock Campbell, the trawler's engineer, came in through the door. Losing his footing, he fell sprawling on the deck.

'Blast this sea,' he cursed as he climbed to his feet with some difficulty. He hastily grabbed the binnacle for support as the trawler staggered under the impact of another wave. He gave Malcolm a tired and worried look. 'Things are going from bad to worse down below, Malcolm. I think we've sprung a leak, just aft of the engine-room. It's not too bad at the moment, but it will get no better in this weather. I've tried to stop it but I can't. I think the old girl is beginning to come apart at the seams.'

Malcolm was alarmed. The engineer was inclined to deal with anything that happened below decks without bothering him. To come to the wheel-house and report the leak meant it must be serious.

'I'd better come down and have a look.' Turning to the man at the wheel, he said, 'Hold the present course, Angus. I'll away and check what's happening below decks. We'll decide what needs to be done when I come back.'

He followed the engineer through the doorway and was away for about twenty minutes. When he crashed back in the wheel-house, there was an anxious expression on his face.

'It's bad. Very bad,' he replied, in answer to Angus's question. 'We'll not make Aberdeen, that's a certainty. In fact, the way water's coming in, we'll be lucky to make a landfall.'

As he was speaking he was pulling charts from a cupboard in the corner of the wheel-house. Studying them for a few moments, he said, 'It looks as though Ardness is our nearest harbour. Have you ever taken a boat in there, Angus?'

The old man shook his head. 'No — but I've heard it said that it has one of the trickiest approaches on this part of the coast. The channel has a great many twists and turns, with some ugly rocks waiting for any boat that strays off course. It's not a good place to make for in this kind of weather.'

Malcolm's face set in a grim expression. 'I'm sure you're right, Angus, but we have no choice. Another hour and we'll have so much water down below it will stop the engines. I don't need to tell you what that would mean in a sea like this.'

Angus nodded, in sober agreement. 'You're the skipper, laddie. It's your decision. If you say we must put in to Ardness, then that's the way it will be. Do you want me to stay at the wheel?'

'Aye. Take her thirty degrees to starboard and we'll need to keep a sharp look-out. We can't be too far away from the Ardness channel.'

The next half an hour was a nightmare. The change of course brought the trawler broadside-on to the storm. Each crashing wave caused the little boat to shudder and roll alarmingly.

Both men were staring hard into the darkness ahead of them. Suddenly, Malcolm clutched Angus's shoulder.

'Did you see anything just then?'

The grizzled helmsman shook his head. 'Only the lightning.'

Malcolm tightened his grip. 'That's when I saw it. I'm sure it was spray — and it was straight ahead. That means rocks. We'd better slow down.'

Another flash of lightning ripped through the storm clouds curtaining the night sky. Malcolm cried out, 'There! You must have seen it that time. It must be rocks. Now, which way do we go? To the left, or the right of them?'

The older man shook his head, perplexed. For

the next few seconds there was an agonising silence in the trawler's wheel-house.

It was broken by an excited shout from Angus. 'Look! Look there, Malcolm — over to starboard. It's another trawler! They must be taking it into Ardness too. All we need do is follow it in.'

He swung the wheel hard over. For a few, heart-stopping moments it seemed the trawler would not respond. Then, slowly and painfully, timbers groaning under the strain, *Bluebell* came around.

There, not fifty yards ahead, were the navigation lights of the other boat, heading in towards the unseen land.

The distance between the two trawlers narrowed and soon they were playing a desperate game of follow-the-leader, with the knowledge that certain death was the penalty for failure. More than once, as lightning lit the sky and *Bluebell* turned this way and that, following the other boat's zig-zag course, Malcolm saw jagged rocks rising from the sea about them.

Then, miraculously, there were no more waves towering around them. They had reached sheltered waters and ahead they could see the lights of a fishing village. As they drew near to the long, stone jetty that reached out in to the salt water loch, Malcolm sounded the trawler's klaxon. The strident blast brought villagers running from their cottages and someone shone a powerful spotlight in the trawler's direction. It was apparent that *Bluebell* was in serious danger of sinking and lanterns were produced to guide the boat to a berth alongside the jetty.

When Malcolm felt his boat ground on the soft mud of the harbour-side, he cut the engines. Minutes later a lattice-work of stout ropes linked boat and jetty. They were safe. Malcolm had saved his boat and the crew. Later, seated by the fireside of the village's waterfront inn, with a large tot of rum inside him and surrounded by a crowd of Ardness fishermen, he remembered the trawler he had followed in to the safety of the harbour. He asked the men about him where he might find the skipper of the trawler, in order to thank him for showing him the channel.

His enquiry was greeted with puzzlement by the local men seated about him.

'You're the only boat to come in to Ardness today,' one of them said. 'All of our fleet returned to harbour yesterday. Besides, there's not an Ardness skipper who'd risk his boat in that channel in darkness and with this sea running.'

'But there *was* a trawler,' insisted Malcolm. 'Had there not been we would never have found our way in. Neither Angus, nor myself, have ever been here before.'

The local fishermen looked at each other uncomfortably. It was quite obvious that although they did not wish to argue with him, they all believed Malcolm had imagined the other trawler.

'I tell you there *was* a boat ahead of us,' Malcolm said, almost angrily. 'Why, I can even tell you its name. I read it during one of the lightning flashes. It was the *Kilross Head*,

202

registered right here in Ardness. You must know it!'

There was a long silence before one of the fishermen, an old man, replied. 'Aye, we know it, laddie. Or, to be more truthful, we *did*.' He paused and pulled a pipe from his pocket. Avoiding Malcolm's puzzled gaze, he made a great show of filling and lighting it.

Looking up at last, he said quietly, 'Were you not telling us just now that you would be marrying an Ardness lass? Young Janie Grant who moved to Aberdeen from here some years ago?'

Malcolm nodded. 'That's right, but what . . . ?'

'Well you see,' said the old man, in his soft voice, 'The *Kilross Head* was her father's boat. He died when she was wrecked on the rocks out there, fifteen years ago this very night.'

Latitude 57.23 North;
Longitude 33.29 West

'Latitude 57.23 North; Longitude 33.29 West, Sir.' The cultured voice of Lieutenant Brady, the ship's Navigating Officer, issuing metallically from the voice-pipe on the bridge, startled the captain and he realised that he must have been nodding off.

'Thank you, Navs,' he called back to the chartroom. 'Get a signal off, will you?'

He ran a weary hand over the stubble on his chin. Hell, he was tired! It was this infernal weather.

Gripping the narrow shelf in front of him, he ducked his head below the level of the bridge as a massive wave bore down upon the tiny minesweeper, approaching with a roar like that of a train emerging from a tunnel. The ship groaned as tons of water cascaded over its forecastle, the strong wind whipping spray high over the bridge. Then, with a bone-jarring shudder and for all the world like a fat old lady heavily laden with parcels, wearily climbing a steep flight of stairs, the ship slowly and laboriously emerged from the wave. But it enjoyed only a brief respite before the next one thundered down upon it.

Raising his head, the Captain automatically looked about him. There was nothing but the huge seas, rising all around the ship in cold, heaving grey slopes.

'I really ought to be used to this,' he told himself, 'after all those years I spent up here.'

But those days were very different. Then he was *Mister* Carson, skipper of his own fishing trawler and no social barrier existed to set him apart from his crew. He was able to curse the sea and they would growl their agreement in return. Now he was Lieutenant Commander Carson, Commanding Officer of Her Majesty's mine-sweeper *Prowler* and, in the loneliness that command carried with it, it was necessary to keep his thoughts to himself.

Thinking back to those earlier days, he was aware they had been harder than this. Not only had there been the daily conflict with the sea, there had been fish to find and net. A living to be made for himself and his crew. Now he had only to ensure his ship's routine ran smoothly. That, and patrol these Arctic waters in case a trawler ran into trouble. Fishery Protection duty it was called. The thought gave him a feeling of great satisfaction. At heart he was still a fisherman.

At the beginning of the last war, he was commissioned into the Royal Navy. Skilful seamanship and an instinctive knowledge of the sea brought him an offer of a permanent commission and he accepted it. Now he was back in the part of the ocean he knew best, in the Arctic fishing waters. Even so, he was aware that he was older and wardroom life had made him soft. He gave a wry smile as he thought about it, then ducked again as another giant wave swept down upon his ship.

Crouching below the rim of the bridge screen,

he saw the other occupant of the bridge doing the same. As he watched, the thin, young face turned towards him, eyes dark above the uneven fuzz of an adolescent beard. Seeing the ghost of a smile on the young man's face, Carson felt a sudden twinge of pity for him. Poor young devil, he thought. Sub-Lieutenant Barton was a well-bred, intelligent lad who should have been gracing the wardroom of some Admiral's yacht, making witty conversation over the rim of a cocktail glass. Instead, he had been posted to *H.M.S. Prowler*.

'Never mind, Sub . . . ' — Carson had to shout to make his voice heard above the howling of the wind — ' . . . this will make a sailor of you.'

He grinned as the youngster pulled a wry face. 'I hope you are right, Sir,' came the reply. 'I was afraid it might put me off the sea for life.'

Further conversation was interrupted by the arrival of the Navigating Officer, heralded by the clatter of heavy sea-boots on the iron ladder leading to the bridge.

Unfortunately, his arrival coincided with that of the next wave. Before he could find something to cling to, his feet skidded on the icy, wet deck and he fell down, each of his legs going in a different direction.

As the ship struggled to right itself he ended in a heap by the flag locker. Rising unsteadily, he ruefully rubbed his head through the double thickness of anorak and duffle-coat. He managed to maintain a tight-lipped silence, but the expression on his bearded face clearly mirrored his thoughts.

'That was quite an entrance, Navs,' said his commanding officer, cheerfully. 'You'll have to teach that one to the Sub. It should prove quite a party piece.'

The Navigating Officer glared at the chuckling Sub-Lieutenant. 'That young man knows all the party pieces already, if the one I saw him with the last time we were in Tromso is a fair example.'

'Ah yes, that reminds me,' said Carson. 'Aren't we due to turn back and head for Tromso soon?'

Lieutenant Brady rummaged in his pockets and eventually located a piece of paper. Holding it over the pale yellow light illuminating the compass, he checked his calculations.

'That's right, sir. Another five hours on our present course and then we turn. I'll give you the new course then.'

Nodding an acknowledgement, Carson looked at his watch. 'Fine. I think I'll go down to my cabin for a couple of hours.'

Turning back to the Sub-Lieutenant, he said, 'Give me a call before we alter course.'

He turned and had one foot on the steel ladder leading down to the wheelhouse when the signal buzzer that linked the wireless office to the bridge sounded. Forced to compete with the noise of the Arctic storm, it was no more than a faint sound, but there was something in its high-pitched note that imparted an indefinable sense of urgency.

Carson paused, bracing himself against the rail

of the ladder while the Sub-Lieutenant drew up a long cord from the voice-pipe leading to the wireless office. At last, he held a small rubber tube connected to the cord and removed the message it contained. As Sub-Lieutenant Barton smoothed out the paper, the Navigating Officer moved to his side and they read it together.

Brady called out something to the Captain. He was unable to make out the words, but the expression on the officer's face told him it must be a matter of some importance. He returned to the bridge, took the message and, crouching by the compass light, read it for himself.

It was chillingly brief and to the point.

'Fishing trawler *Lady Miriam* of Hull reports engine failure in very heavy seas. Immediate assistance is requested.' The terse message ended with the position of the trawler.

Lieutenant Commander Carson straightened up, all thoughts of rest forgotten. He tried to remember the position he had recently signalled. How far away was the trawler? How long would it take to reach her? Even more important, how long could the stricken vessel remain afloat? Turning to Lieutenant Brady, he ordered, 'Work out our relative positions and give me a course to take in order to reach the *Lady Miriam*.'

Dismissing him, he spoke to Barton. 'Get all heads of department to my cabin — immediately!'

★   ★   ★

211

The small group of men waited uncomfortably in the captain's cabin, each leaning against something as a support to counteract the movement of the ship. The door opened and the engineer officer came in, murmuring his apologies. He had been in the engine-room when he received the Captain's summons. Dressed in overalls and carrying heavy, oil-stained gloves, he brought with him a nauseous odour of fuel oil.

Lieutenant Commander Carson put them quickly in the picture. 'We've received a message to say there's a trawler in trouble, not too far away from us. Their engine has failed — and you can all imagine what that means in this weather.'

The assembled men nodded, understanding the plight of the fishermen only too well.

'We are going to their assistance,' continued Carson. 'I'm just waiting for the Navigating Officer to give me a course. When I get it we'll decide what's to be done.'

There was a knock at the door and Lieutenant Brady entered the cabin. He looked at the Commanding Officer and, in response to his nod, said, 'I estimate we are about a hundred and five, or a hundred and ten miles from the trawler. In this sea we won't be able to make much more than ten knots. So we should be somewhere near them in about ten hours or so.'

The Captain was lost in his own thoughts. In ten hours' time the fishermen on their stricken trawler might be dead, victims of the merciless Arctic Ocean. On the other hand, to attempt to reach them earlier might endanger his own ship. It was a difficult decision, but one that no one else could make for him.

He stood up and after gazing thoughtfully at the waiting men, said to Lieutenant Brady, 'Send a signal that we are proceeding to their assistance at all possible speed. I estimate we will be in their vicinity six hours from now.'

Turning to the engineer officer, he asked, 'Do you think we can maintain sufficient speed to do it?'

Transferring his gloves from one hand to the other, the engineer officer shrugged and said, 'You tell me what speed you want to maintain and I'll ensure the engines keep running. Whatever it is, it can't be fast enough for those poor devils out there waiting for someone to come to their aid.'

Lieutenant Commander Carson nodded approval. 'Good. The rest of you let the crew know what's happening. I shall want scrambling nets rigged along both sides — and make certain they are properly secured. We're probably going to need them. Oh . . . and we'll need look-outs on the bridge too. It seems the radar is on the blink again . . . '

The radar had been playing up for some time. Replacement parts from England should have reached them before now.

As the men filed from the cabin, Carson called up to the Sub-Lieutenant on the bridge and gave him the new course to steer. Then he went out on deck to watch the seamen who were already pulling scramble-nets from lockers.

With a sudden lurch, the ship yawed as she swung to her new course, the throb of the powerful engines taking on a new note as the ship increased speed.

The ship would now be running broadside on to the sea and it would make life on board extremely uncomfortable while the course was held.

A sample of what the next few hours would be like came while Carson was making his way forward to the bridge. A huge wave crashed down on the ship with terrifying strength and he was forced to fling his arms around a stanchion to prevent himself from being washed overboard. As he clung to the slim, iron pillar he heard a splintering of wood from a ship's boat, hanging amidships. From the wardroom there was the sound of smashing crockery as cupboard doors burst open, spewing out cups, plates and dishes.

It took him much longer than usual to reach the bridge, but once there he immediately countermanded his orders concerning the scrambling nets. He would find time to have them rigged when they found the trawler. It was not necessary to risk the lives of his crew under the present conditions. Instead, he issued orders for the crew to remain below decks.

The following six hours were nightmarish. All the ship's boats on the starboard side were reduced to matchwood by the pounding seas. Meanwhile, a boat on the port side threshed about wildly, secured by only one davit, smashing everything within its pendulous range.

But still H.M.S. Prowler maintained speed, in spite of the conditions — and they were worse than anyone on board had experienced before.

One minute the ship pursued a corkscrew course through the sea; the next the stern would rise clear of the water, the ship's screws spinning wildly and noisily.

Eventually, the minesweeper arrived at the last known position of the trawler and Carson was able to order a reduction in speed as they began a search of the area. On the bridge, an anxious group of men strained their eyes into the Arctic gloom, ignoring icy spray that settled on their faces, decorating their beards with a myriad of frosty needles.

There was nothing to be seen. Nothing but the omnipresent waves towering about them, and the subdued colours of *Aurora Borealis*, flickering eerily above the heaving skyline and Carson cursed the faulty radar.

He kept his hopes alive with the knowledge that the trawler might be over the next wave, invisible to the men on the minesweeper until they were on top of it.

This was exactly what happened. One minute there was nothing; the next, as they rode the crest of a wave, they saw the trawler sliding into the trough ahead of them. Everyone on the bridge saw it at the same time and there was not a man among them who was not filled with amazement that the small vessel remained afloat.

Lady Miriam was in a bad way. The mast had broken away flush with the deck, and boats and fishing tackle had been swept away. In fact, there was nothing left above deck except a tiny wheelhouse. Through gaping windows which had once contained glass, the crew could be seen huddling together.

Somehow they had managed to rig up a sea-anchor; a long canvas bag like a huge bucket attached to the end of a cable which stretched out into the sea. This alone had kept the trawler bows-on to the running sea, preventing them from being turned over and sent to the bottom of the ocean. Even so, they could not last much longer. The trawler had shipped a lot of water and was riding dangerously low in the water.

The distressed vessel had been found — but this was not the end of *Prowler's* mission. The crew had to be rescued, somehow. It would not be easy. Lieutenant Commander Carson decided this was not the time to attempt elaborate rescue methods. What was needed was seamanship, purely and simply.

Turning to Lieutenant Brady, he ordered, 'Get those scrambling-nets out on the starboard side — now! Have as many men as possible on the same side. Tell them to wear life-lines, tied to something secure. They are to grab the crew of the trawler and haul them inboard as they come across to us. I'm going alongside.'

Brady, himself a first class seaman, realised the enormity of the task. This was not to be the simple coming alongside of one ship to another. This would be the meeting of two wildly pitching ships in a treacherous sea. If the ships came together too quickly — and it was difficult to see how this could be avoided — there would be the terrifying rending of metal as plates parted and neither ship might ever return to harbour. The whole operation would depend upon the skill of the man at the wheel. It would be a fearfully daunting task.

As though Carson had read the navigator's thoughts, he said, 'Jump to it, Navs. I shall want you here on the bridge. I'll be taking the wheel myself.'

His voice was crisp and unemotional, showing none of the fierce tension that gripped him.

Brady was startled. He was something of a naval historian and could recall no occasion when a Commanding Officer of a warship had taken the wheel, whatever the emergency. Nevertheless, he hurried away to carry out the Captain's orders.

* * *

All was ready on the starboard side, the sailors waiting, tense and expectant.

Lieutenant Commander Carson was at the wheel, the ship's coxwain beside him, hands poised over the telegraphs. He was ready to signal changes of engine speed to the engineer officer far below, in the bowels of the ship.

The minesweeper and the trawler were close together now, the minesweeper slightly ahead and to the side of the other vessel.

Carson peered over his shoulder through the spray running down the windows of the wheelhouse. Gauging his distance, he snapped out a constant stream of orders.

Slowly, the distance between the two ships lessened. Thirty yards; twenty yards . . . ten. Now they were level, only a few yards of wildly undulating sea separating them.

Swinging the wheel rapidly, first one way and then the other, Carson brought the minesweeper ever closer to the trawler. Now there was no sea to be seen between them. For one long second, it appeared to his anxiously watching crew that he had misjudged the distance.

The trawler, its decks awash, had disappeared below the level of the minesweeper. Then, as the naval men held their breath in fearful anticipation of the seemingly inevitable crash, it appeared again — and the first two fishermen jumped across the narrow gap separating the two vessels.

Sailors rushed forward to grab them and pull them to safety.

Carson swung the wheel again. This time the ships did meet, but it was no more than a glancing blow — and three more fishermen reached safety.

The next time the ships came together with more force. Much more force. Twenty feet of the minesweeper's guard-rail was carried away and one of the bridge supports was severely bent.

The collision caused mortal damage to the trawler. As the two ships fell away from each other, Carson could see a gaping hole in the side of the *Lady Miriam*.

But it did not matter now. During the last, violent collision, the last of the fishermen had jumped to safety. The trawler would plunge to the bed of the deep ocean crewless. A cage from which the birds had escaped in the nick of time.

The Arctic Ocean had been robbed of its intended victims.

Putting on speed, the minesweeper hauled well clear of the stricken trawler. A wave thundered up between them and, when it subsided, *Lady Miriam* had disappeared.

Handing over control of the wheel to the coxwain, Lieutenant Commander Carson left the wheelhouse and made his way to the bridge. The strain of the recent ordeal was plain to see on his face and he smiled tired-eyed at the men who showered congratulations on him.

'Thank you, gentlemen,' he said, emotionally. 'Will you convey my thanks to all members of crew. I am proud of them.'

Addressing Lieutenant Brady, he said, 'Navs, will you plot a course for Tromso? I think we need to put in for repairs and a few days' rest for the crew.'

'Oh yes . . . ' he added, as the Navigating Officer was about to turn away. 'Will you ask the skipper of the trawler to join me for a drink in my cabin? His name is Carson. Arthur Carson.'

There was a surprised silence from the men on the bridge and Lieutenant Commander Carson smiled apologetically. 'No,' he explained, 'it's no coincidence. Arthur is my brother.'

He turned away, gazing out over the harsh, unfeeling sea, so that none of the men could see his expression. When he spoke again his words were almost inaudible above the sound of the wind and the crashing of the sea.

'The *Lady Miriam* belonged to my family. She used to be *my* ship.'

There was a long silence and when he turned to the others again, his face was wet with what might have been spray.

'Yes, Navs. Ask my brother to come and join me and tell him . . . Tell him . . . I am very pleased to have him aboard.'

Opportunity Knocks

The decision that would change the course of Arnold Fingelstein's life was made in a small cafe, a mere rumble away from Liverpool Street Station. It came just as the cup of tea on the table before him celebrated two cold hours of existence.

Coming to grips with problems was no new experience for Arnold. In show business, problems came more readily than did work — especially for impersonators. At the mere mention of the word 'impersonations' a theatrical agent would sigh deeply and produce a photograph album containing the pictures of fifty other impersonators, their names and details gathering dust in his ancient card index system. It counted for nothing that your characterisations of Clinton, Yeltsin, Blair and a host of others were better than the real thing. The market was overloaded with impersonators, both male and female.

That was why Arnold decided to change his act. He had thought about it for a long time. Too long. It was now time to take action. Taking the cold tea by surprise, Arnold downed it in one long, distasteful gulp, before setting off into the night.

Back at his shabby room, Arnold straddled a chair in front of the cracked mirror hanging above the wash-basin and tried to produce intelligible speech without moving his lips. He had decided to become a ventriloquist and continue doing impressions through the medium of a dummy. It was the first of many hundreds of hours Arnold was to spend in front of a mirror. He practised until he could reproduce the voice he wanted without the slightest trace of lip movement.

With time, he became good — exceptionally good. One night he had a policeman frantically searching shop doorways in Oxford Street for a baby that would not stop crying. On another occasion, he left a near-hysterical crowd on a suburban train begging a panting bulldog to repeat the Churchillian speech it had just made.

But there was still one thing missing in Arnold Fingelstein's life. He needed a dummy — a really good one — with which to launch his career. But such items were made only by highly skilled craftsmen — and they were very expensive. He would need a bank loan in order to purchase one. Fortunately, he had maintained a bank account, against a 'rainy day'. The amount invested usually hovered about the five pound mark, but it proved sufficient to secure an introduction to the bank manager.

Arnold's bank was the sole survivor of a once thriving row of shops and business houses. It hardly warranted its staff of three, but certain formalities were still strictly observed. He was ushered into the manager's office and waved to a leather chair. Across the desk from him was a man who exuded the quiet authority that sets bank managers apart from mere mortals.

'Well now, Mr Fingelstein.' The face looking down at Arnold's banking record wore a somewhat puzzled expression. 'And what can I do for you?'

'I want a bank loan,' replied Arnold, brightly.

The expression deepened to a frown. 'I see! Perhaps you would care to tell me about it.'

When Arnold finished his explanation, the bank manager looked at him in undisguised astonishment.

'You want a bank loan, Mr Fingelstein . . . for a doll?'

'A dummy,' Arnold corrected him. 'An essential item to set myself up in business as a self-employed entertainer. I can assure you, it would be an excellent investment. Why, the loan would be outstanding for no more than a year. I might even be able to repay it in less time than that.'

'That's as may be, Mister Fingelstein, but can you imagine the reaction of the auditor at head office when he checked the books and saw I had loaned the bank's money to buy a *doll* — call it what I may. I would become a laughing stock in banking circles!'

'I can assure you, Sir, I — '

There was a sudden and unexpected interruption in the shape of a well-dressed man who opened the door and burst into the office, closely pursued by the protesting girl cashier who had shown Arnold in.

'I'm sorry,' she apologised unhappily to the manager. 'I told this gentleman you were busy, but he said his business wouldn't wait.'

'Please don't blame the young lady,' said the stranger, politely, in a cultured voice. 'It's my fault entirely. But I'm desperately pushed for time and my business won't take more than a couple of minutes.'

'This really is *most* irregular,' bristled the manager. 'I don't know what the world is coming to. First I'm asked for money to buy a doll, and now this . . . All right, Miss Dickson, back to your work. I will deal with this.'

As the door closed behind her, the manager said, 'Now, sir, I must ask you to — '

The manager halted in mid-sentence.

With the casual air of a man unwrapping sandwiches in a park, the stranger opened the briefcase he was carrying and plunged his hand inside.

It emerged holding a revolver.

The gun barrel pointed at the bank manager before shifting in Arnold's direction.

'Get over there.'

Arnold moved hastily to stand beside the bank manager.

'Good! Now, if we are all sensible, nobody will get hurt.'

Speaking to the manager, he said, 'I am going to place this gun in my pocket — but my hand will stay there with it, of course. Furthermore, my finger will be on the trigger and I must warn you, it begins to twitch with the passing of time, so you had better be quick. You will pick up the telephone — the internal one — and tell your cashier to bring in ten thousand pounds. No more and no less. I am not a greedy man.'

As the bank manager's mouth opened and closed silently, the gunman showed his first trace of nervousness.

'I mean NOW, before I lose control of my twitching finger!'

The manager's hand darted out towards the telephone, but paused when there came a knock at the door.

As the gunman swung around to look in that direction, a gruff voice called out, 'You, in there! This is the police. Put down your gun and come out quietly.'

It was the gunman's turn to look dumbfounded.

The knock was repeated and a second voice called, 'You heard my sergeant. I have the bank surrounded by armed police — and I am not prepared to negotiate with you. Put down your gun and surrender. If you force me to send in my men they'll come in shooting.'

As the gunman hesitated, the door handle turned slowly.

'All right! I give up. Don't shoot!'

The would-be robber dropped the gun on the desk as the door slowly opened.

The next moment the nervous girl cashier put her head around the door.

Arnold beat the other man to the gun by only a fraction of a second — but it was enough. When the police arrived in answer to the manager's alarm call, the gunman was crouched disconsolately in a corner of the office, his hands clasped firmly on top of his head.

'That was quite remarkable!' said the bank

manager to Arnold, as the police escorted their prisoner to a waiting car. 'You had me completely fooled. I could have sworn those voices came from outside the door.'

'It was fortunate your cashier knocked at the door when she did,' said Arnold. 'But we mustn't forget the reason I was here in the first place. Do I get the bank loan?'

'Bank loan? My dear chap . . . '

The bank manager led Arnold to a notice-board on the wall of his office. A handbill pinned to it declared that the clearing banks would pay a reward leading to the conviction of anyone involved in a bank robbery.

The reward ran into five figures.

'I think your query is with our Investments department, Mr Fingelstein, not with Loans. While we are talking of the future, may I reserve two front seats for your first appearance at the Palladium . . . ?'

The Last of Her Line

Wendy St Gerard was frightened — and the servants of the ancient manor house were frightened for her. She was aware of it by the way they avoided looking directly at her whenever they entered a room where she was.

She was seated on the wide window-seat in the old, panelled lounge, knees drawn up to her chin. Outside was a blanket of grey sea fog. It had rolled in with the tide that morning and quickly swallowed up the whole of the West Cornwall peninsula. It was the depressing, damp fog which made everything seem so much worse. Had she been able to look out upon sun-drenched lawns and watch waves rolling in to disintegrate upon the tall, grey cliffs, things would somehow have seemed so much more normal. At least, as normal as any day could possibly be when there had been a sighting of the galleon.

Tears glistened in eyes that appeared so much darker against the pallor of her face, but they remained trembling on her lashes. Pride would not let them take their course. Yet Wendy was more frightened than she had ever been before. She was angry too. Angry that the galleon and its centuries-old curse should fill her with such terror. All because she had been born a St Gerard. The last surviving member of an old Cornish family.

The legend of the galleon had been with the family for more than three hundred years, although no one really knew when or why it had come about. The only thing that was not in doubt was that it had never failed to herald a death in the family.

The galleon, sails furled, had appeared the night her grandfather had been shot down and killed over Germany, during the last months of the war. It had been a bright, moonlit night and the apparition had been sighted by three fishermen, working on the jetty. It had appeared again when her only brother had died in a motor car accident. Then there had been the night, only two years before, when her father lay in his bed in the house, seriously ill. A young housemaid had seen it on that occasion. Courting on the cliff edge, she had deserted her lover and ran back to the house, almost hysterical. 'Not two hundred yards from the shore, it was,' cried the frightened young woman. 'Sailing by with not a living soul on board. Awful, it was. I've never ever seen anything like it.' The young girl had then given way to a bout of uncontrollable weeping. Sir Hugh St Gerard had died in the early hours of the next morning, leaving Wendy as the sole survivor of the once proud family.

Now the galleon had returned once more, that very morning — and it was under full sail. It had appeared to be heading straight for the small fishing village at the mouth of the valley, below where the big house stood. The postman had seen it, so too had Mrs Trelawney from the little village shop. As is the way with small communities, the news of the sighting went around the village within minutes. Now, the superstitious villagers waited in their cottages for the final chapter of the St Gerard's family history to be written.

The words of the legend were written in the flyleaf of the ancient, leather-bound history book that lay on the seat beside Wendy.

She knew the words by heart:

When, sails reeved in and pennant high,
The galleon's seen by mortal eye,
Then one St Gerard more must die.
But when it's seen with full sails o'er,
St Gerard's name shall be no more.

The fog swirled over the lawns in front of the window and Wendy shivered. She felt that if she stayed in the house for many more hours, she would go out of her mind. The answer would be to seek the company of people her own age. Friends who did not know of the legend and, even if they were told of it, would laugh it off.

But the only close friends she had these days were in London, where she worked in a publishing house during the week, returning to Cornwall only at weekends. She looked at her watch and wondered whether she might make it to London before nightfall? The fog would slow her, of course, but the television weather forecaster seemed to think it was a local phenomenon only. She decided she could comfortably make the journey and felt better immediately.

She tugged at the bell-pull beside the fireplace. A maid appeared within a few moments.

'Lucille, pack my suitcase for me. I'm returning to London right away. Hurry now. Oh, and have my car brought around to the front of the house, please.'

Jumping to her feet, Wendy prepared herself for the journey. She was an extremely attractive girl and the trouser suit she chose to wear showed off her figure to advantage.

The servants were gathered around the door as she climbed into the small, red sports car. A roar of the engine, a quick wave of her hand and she pulled away, the car quickly disappearing in the fog.

'Poor dear,' said the cook, 'She'm trying to get away from the curse of the galleon, but 'er won't, you mark my words. None of the St Gerards has escaped it yet. 'Tis an awful shame, her being such an attractive maid, but I fear we'm seen the last of the St Gerards. You just see if I ain't right.'

So saying, she turned and went inside the house, shaking her head sadly.

⋆　⋆　⋆

The fog persisted for about ten miles before disappearing and Wendy was able to put her foot down on the accelerator and the little car sped on its way to London. She had been travelling for almost three hours when she decided to leave the motorway and have a meal at a small inn she had visited a couple of times before. She came over the brow of the hill at the very moment that a tractor towing a laden trailer pulled out of a field. It was impossible to avoid a collision. The sound of screeching brakes and rending metal reached the residents of a nearby village, and then there was an ominous silence. The small red sports car, almost a total wreck, lay upon its side in a ditch. Wendy's still figure was sprawled on the verge not far away.

★   ★   ★

Every villager gathered for the service in the small Cornish church. Not one was absent. They were all aware that this simple ceremony would bring the house of St Gerard to an end. It would be remembered only in plaques about the walls and in the inscriptions beneath the reclining stone statues in various corners of the building. The name that had founded a village would be no more.

The organist pressed on the keys of his instrument and, as deep sound filled the church, the congregation rose to their feet.

The notes swelled and grew — and down the aisle came Wendy, looking as radiant as a bride should on such an occasion.

The tall, dark, intelligent-looking young man standing at the front of the church, a carnation adorning his lapel, could not resist a quick glance over his shoulder at the bride.

'Did you see that look?' whispered the cook, to a housemaid. 'Ah, 'tis a fine bridegroom that Miss Wendy's getting. Mind you, she'm some lucky that he came along right after the accident,

235

him being a surgeon and all.'

She wiped a romantic tear from her cheek. 'Mind you, 'tis sad to see the name of St Gerard disappearing for ever, but I really can't think of a nicer way for it to happen.'

THE END

We do hope that you have enjoyed reading this large print book.

Did you know that all of our titles are available for purchase?

We publish a wide range of high quality large print books including:
Romances, Mysteries, Classics
General Fiction
Non Fiction and Westerns

Special interest titles available in large print are:
The Little Oxford Dictionary
Music Book
Song Book
Hymn Book
Service Book

Also available from us courtesy of Oxford University Press:
Young Readers' Dictionary
(large print edition)
Young Readers' Thesaurus
(large print edition)

For further information or a free brochure, please contact us at:
Ulverscroft Large Print Books Ltd.,
The Green, Bradgate Road, Anstey,
Leicester, LE7 7FU, England.
Tel: **(00 44) 0116 236 4325**
Fax: **(00 44) 0116 234 0205**

Other titles in the
Charnwood Library Series:

FALLING SLOWLY

Anita Brookner

Beatrice and Miriam are sisters, loving but not entirely uncritical; each secretly deplores the other's aspirations. Their lives fall short of what they would have wished for themselves: love, intimacy, exclusivity, acknowledgement in the eyes of the world, even a measure of respect. Each discovers to her cost that love can be a self-seeking business and that lovers have their own exclusive desires. In search of reciprocity, the sisters are forced back into each other's company, and rediscover their original closeness.

THE LADY ON MY LEFT

Catherine Cookson

Alison Read, orphaned when she was two years old, had for some years lived and worked with Paul Aylmer, her appointed guardian. Paul, an experienced antique dealer whose business thrived in the south-coast town of Sealock, had come to rely on Alison, who had quickly learned the trade. But when he had asked her to value the contents of Beacon Ride, a chain of events was set off that led to the exposure of a secret he had for years managed to conceal. As a result, Alison's relationship with Paul came under threat and she knew that only by confronting the situation head-on would her ambitions be realised.

FLIGHT OF EAGLES

Jack Higgins

In 1997 a wealthy novelist, his wife and their pilot are forced to ditch in the English Channel. Saved by a lifeboat crew, they are returned to land at Cold Harbour. But it is the rediscovery of a fighter pilot's lucky mascot — unseen for half a century — that excites the greatest interest at the disused airbase. The mascot's owners, twin brothers Max and Harry Kelso, were separated as boys and found themselves fighting on opposite sides when the Second World War broke out. They were to meet again under amazing circumstances — and upon their actions hung the fate of the war itself . . .